A
Butler
Summer

A Butler Summer

Rahiem Brooks

PRODIGY GOLD BOOKS

PHILADELPHIA * LOS ANGELES

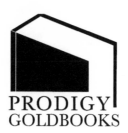

PRODIGY
GOLDBOOKS

A BUTLER SUMMER

A Prodigy Gold Book

Prodigy Gold E-book edition / July 2018

Prodigy Gold Paperback edition / July 2018

Copyright (c) 2018 by Rahiem Brooks

Library of Congress Catalog Card Number: 2017

Website: http://www.prodigygoldbooks.com

Author's e-mail: rahiembthewriter@gmail.com

Editor: Locksie Locks

ISBN 978-1-939665-26-3

Published simultaneously in the US and Canada

PRINTED IN THE UNITED STATES OF AMERICA

A
Butler
Summer

CHAPTER 1

SUNDAY

New York, NY—Hector's Brazilian Bistro

Sunday evening, Naim Butler, Derrick Adams, and their depression settled into their regular corner four-top at Hector's Brazilian Bistro. Their favorite waitress dropped off champagne glasses and a bucket with chilled bottles of their favorite stress medication: Dom Perignon coupled with shots of Ciroc red-berry vodka. They enjoyed the therapeutic concoction while reflecting on their eventful day.

Easing through their second dose, they were joined by Hector, the restaurant's namesake and their close friend. He threw them a suspicious smile. "Well, aren't you two on your sartorial worse. Costumes? It's only August."

"On-demand movers," Naim said, smiling, raising his eyebrows. He cocked his head to the side.

"We delivered the boys to Columbia today to start their freshman year. They're the school's problem now," said Derrick, laughing.

"Good, it's not Halloween?" Hector said. "Dumped them off at college, so now your misery begins. Drink up."

"How?" Naim asked, pouring himself another Perignon/Ciroc mix.

"Empty-nest heartache," Hector said. "And good luck with the thoughts of what they'll be doing. *Jesus*. Do you recall our freshman year at Tulane?"

"I was fucking my brains out," Naim replied.

"As was I," added Derrick, sipping and chuckling.

"And remember, I've been a dad barely nine months, so I'll manage," Naim said.

"Still can't believe Sinia didn't tell you that she had a baby by you for seventeen-damn-years. Tragedy," Hector said, shaking his head.

"Indeed. Grateful that we're over that. He has to reside on campus for his freshman year, but he lives in the former maid quarters attached to my house—"

"Mini-manse," Derrick said, interrupting him. "Where you live is hardly described as a house."

"Words are powerful," Naim said sarcastically. "Has anyone ever told you how impeccable you are with words?"

"Well, a judge or two complimented me on my closing."

"You're an ass," Hector said, laughing.

"That he is," Naim said. "What prosecutor isn't? I'll be teaching a Criminal Law class at Columbia, too, so I'll be on the campus keeping an eye on my boy."

"Now you're a spy?" Derrick asked, laughing. "First you get a license to practice law, and now you're an investigator."

"Better than all of those clowns investigating at your office."

"You two are crazy," Hector said. He stood and asked, "What are you two eating tonight? After moving stuff all day, I know you're famished."

"Something healthy for us," Derrick said, "because I'm trying to lose my gut."

"I have a six percent body fat, so he's speaking for himself," Naim said. "I'll have a fully-loaded Hawaiian flatbread pizza. Give him water and a Hydroxy Cut Black pill."

They laughed and Hector walked away in time to avoid a tall, almond-hued, bottle-blonde in an expertly tailored Chanel tweed suit. She was headed for their table. Arriving she sat. "Well, hello, boys," Sinia Love said, leering a little.

Naim furrowed his brows. "Hello, Sinia. We're men by the way."

"Tomatoe. Tomatah," she replied, rolling her eyes.

"What brings you into this fine restaurant?" Naim asked. A large gulp of vodka straight from the bottle followed the question.

"This *is* where the New York upper-assholes, oops, I meant, Upper East Siders, that can afford to eat here hang out, right?"

"I live in Brooklyn," Derrick said flatly, sipping his cocktail.

"Then I'm not referring to you, right?" Sarcastic smirk followed an exaggerated wink.

Her emphasis of the word *right* crawled beneath Derrick's skin. "Let's start over," he said, clasping his hands together. "Why are you here?"

"Not to see you," Sinia replied.

3

The last time she had been in Hector's, she created a Broadway musical scene, and was asked to leave.

To Naim, she said, "I need to hire an attorney of the criminal defense kind." She gently pat Naim's hand. "I need to hire *you* because—"

"Wait," Naim said, holding up a hand. He pinched his bushy eyebrows together and blinked uncontrollably. "I cannot discuss a case, rather, a potential case, in front of a prosecutor. Ethics and privilege conundrum." He had only passed the bar exam months ago, but he knew that much.

"How sad your life must be, Naim. I mean, a prosecutor for a best friend has to be miserable," she said, curling her lips, and throwing eye-daggers at Derrick.

"No, what's sad is…You being the *sad* mother of his child, I'll contain my atrocious comments out of respect for Naim and Marco, but know—" Derrick began as the waitress placed plates on the table interrupting him.

The waitress asked, "Can I get something for you, ma'am?"

Sinia stood and said, "No, I was just going."

"Thank God," Derrick said.

Ignoring him, she looked down at Naim, and said, "I'll be at your *home* office tomorrow at ten-thirty a.m."

"No, you'll call my secretary tomorrow and schedule an appointment," Naim replied, tucking a cloth napkin into the collar of his T-shirt.

"Look at you all professional and stuff. You've always had epic etiquette." She playfully tapped his shoulder. "I won't be handled by your people like I'm a stranger."

"Perhaps you've forgotten, your boyfriend held me, our son, and our dates at gunpoint in my home. Our son killed your lover. Ring a bell?" Naim asked, smiling.

"If Marco wasn't under eighteen and unable to make his own decisions, you'd have a restraining order lodged against you," the prosecutor added.

"Naim," she said, clutching imaginary pearls. "Is this how you allow a man to talk to your child's mother? Does the pathetic prosecutor talk to Brandy Scott with such venom?"

Both men were amazed at her animation. She was an aloof, uncreative woman, and quite predictable. This new person was a bit much.

"Sinia...Sinia," Naim said, frowning. "Tomorrow, I have to teach and I have other engagements, so you will call my secretary. Or not. Your call. But you're not welcome to my home." Another scorching gulp of vodka. Pain spread across his face.

"Trespassing is a crime in New York City," the prosecutor said, biting into a crunchy slice of vegetable flatbread pizza to punctuate the threat.

"Congrats on the professorship, Naim," she said, ignoring Derrick again. "Your class is at eight a.m. You have a conference at Baker and Keefe at eleven-thirty. I'll be at your office, your home office at ten. Toodles." She pivoted and walked away.

"How'd she know your schedule?" Derrick asked.

"Your guess is as good as mine."

"Not quite. My guess involves nefarious methods. Hacking. Home invasion. Crimes that I'd go above and beyond to lock her ass under the jail for committing."

CHAPTER 2

MONDAY

Washington, D.C.—Supreme Court of the United States

Monday morning David Thurman walked along First Street Northeast in Washington, D.C. He was a towering man, stopping in front of the United States Supreme Court, wearing a dark denim blazer that concealed a brass Henry Arms Big Boy Lever Action Centerfire .44-caliber rifle. Climbing three of the eight marble steps, leading to the court's entrance, he shifted a briefcase from one hand to the other. The case didn't contain legal briefs to present to the highest court or any papers at all. It did hide two more weapons—a Sig Sauer MPX 9mm pistol and a Ruger LC9 9mm. *Trained to go!*

A class of high schoolers crowded the Court's elevated marble plaza: an oval terrace spanning two hundred fifty-two feet long and ninety-eight feet wide, paved in gray and white marble in a pattern of alternating circles and squares similar to the Roman Pantheon's floor. All of the students donned business attire, visiting from Germantown High School's Law and Government Magnet Program in Philadelphia, Pennsylvania. David Thurman watched the future *Philadelphia lawyers* marvel at the plaza's two fountains and two flag poles. He had a seat on one of the six marble benches next to an elderly couple. He counted the steps that ascended from the plaza to the building's portico, leading to the magnificent bronze doors that served as the main entrance into the building. Thirty-six. A low wall surrounded the plaza and encircled the rest of the building, providing cover for an assault on the building that sat across the street.

The United States Capitol.

Thurman, an ex-army captain—dishonorably eighty-sixed—gazed indifferently at patriots and visitors taking pictures of the famous buildings. They took selfies for social media postings to chronicle their visit to the world's most powerful capital. *Stupid ingrates,* he thought with little effort disguising his disgust for their enthusiasm. *Imbeciles, blind patriotism, just ignorant fools everywhere, including, these old cows next to me.*

The elderly man caught Thurman staring at him and nodded. The man had no idea that he had spoken to a killing machine. Thurman was the lone gunman in the attack on a New York City police precinct. Thirteen officers were murdered. Ten men. Three women. Four rookies. He smiled at the memory. *Palatable.*

Since then, he had continued to make a name for himself amongst blood-thirsty media hounds with attacks on other police targets in Cleveland, Indianapolis, Detroit, Chicago, and St. Louis—his swing through the Midwest. It was time to feed American's fear of home-grown terror right in Washington, D.C. His new targets were a justice of *the* Court and a U.S. Senator. Both of them had two things in common.

One, they were African-American Democrats.

Two, they were against criminal justice reform.

This may be the end of my murderous roller-coaster ride. Successful or not, the psychological-fear resulting from what he planned was more important than the outcome. Surely, a clean-cut, freckle-faced, blue-eyed, redhead could kill at will, thanks to media clowns. The bogeyman of home-grown radical Islamic terrorists was out of place in the capital—and airports, train stations, office parties, university campuses, gay clubs, and coffee shops. Thurman however, had carte blanche to do as he pleased without racial or religious scrutiny. *Ah, the privilege of being white in America.*

Thurman's musings were interrupted when a United States Capitol Police officer's car passed. The sight caused the killer to smile. The policeman moved fifteen miles per hour. An easy target for the expert marksman. Two tours in Iraq and one in Afghanistan gave him ample opportunity to practice. *Practice makes perfect.*

He brushed beads of sweat from his brows and glanced nervously at a young Asian man strolling by with earbuds in his ears. The man was in his own world and minding his business. *I should kill you first, then, the Capitol policeman. Top that off with the old couple and the high schoolers. But I won't.* Bigger fish in the sea!

CHAPTER 3

New York, New York—Columbia University

Columbia University, an Ivy League powerhouse with a corpulent endowment, and an exceptional law school had hired a dark-chocolate hued, pearly-white teethed, legal eagle, Naim Butler. Born in the Chicago, Illinois slums, he graduated summa cum laude and class valedictorian with a combined bachelors and masters from Tulane University. He graduated with honors from his law school class at the University of Pennsylvania, where he was the editor of the law review and received the Benjamin Jones Award for Public Service. Though he earned a living as a professor of law at Columbia U, it was the Law Offices of Baker and Keefe that monopolized the lion's share of his professional livelihood. For the past two years, he had been a partner of Manhattan's second-largest firm, despite not being licensed to practice law. His specialty sentencing mitigation, an area that he dutifully contributed to the firm as an excellent investigator (sometimes sleuth), legal researcher and writer.

Last spring, though, he earned a Ph.D. at Yale University and finally had the sitting senior New York senator request—as quid pro quo—the sitting United States president, Jackson Radcliffe, to pardon him for committing fraud crimes as a young adult. The president obliged, Naim aced the bar exam and was set to rack up acquittals as a defense attorney—particularly in the United States District Court for the Southern District of New York.

He owned dozens of suits and was in a sleek, pinstriped, blue number, sitting in the third row of a large Columbia lecture hall. He was amongst the students that he was set to teach the art of garnering lenient sentences. Sentencing Mitigation 305.

His mentor, Max Devers, the law school's associate dean continued introducing Dr. Naim Butler. "You ladies and gents have the honor to be the first group taught by a man who rewrote the sentencing mitigation rules. His playbook is as deep as Bill Belichick's, but Naim has a better record. Below guidelines sentences were granted one hundred percent of the times, Butler was on the case. That's why I brought him aboard. Defense attorneys must be prepared to effectively highlight the upbringing, education level, and psychological background of their clients. Oftentimes we fail to adequately and uniquely mitigate for our clients—especially the poor ones—but Butler has the tools to help you all master this. Amazing, right?" Applause from eager students filled the room as Devers let that sink in. "At Baker and Keefe, Butler worked under me at the prestigious firm. A firm that some of you are headed; and, a word from Professor Butler would go a long way to achieve that." Bright smiles spread across the student's faces. Going from college to Baker and Keefe was like going from high school to the NBA. It was reserved for a select few. "Without further delay, Professor Naim Butler," he said over a quiet applause.

Students looked at the huge stage expecting their lecturer to magically appear from behind the curtain. *Tada*. He didn't. Naim stood from amongst their ranks and casually strolled to the stage. Whispers were followed by another applause.

"Thank you," he said as they settled down. His baritone voice was clean and concise. "My first time teaching. Truly honored. Who would have bet on me accomplishing this? One person for sure, the attorney that argued to a federal judge to give me a chance to relocate from Chicago to New Orleans to attend Tulane…"

Boos boomed around the room at the mention of the rival university, causing him to chuckle.

"Tough crowd," he said, smiling. "Know that I am tough, too. Very. Mediocrity and I are mortal enemies, and with that said, let's get to it. You've all been e-mailed syllabus and sample client profiles crafted for you to come up with mitigating arguments to garner them lower sentences. Why, because ninety percent of your cases will result in guilty plea negotiations and require sound sentencing strategies; ergo, it is imperative to be creative and innovative during the sentencing phase. The best hostage negotiator wins. Yes, hostages, because with criminal sentences run amuck, defendants are akin to hostages used as political election talking points from criminal justice reform, but nothing significant has been done to move the ball on that front since 1994. And what significant criminal reform act occurred in 1994?"

Hands shot up in the air. Naim consulted his seating chart and picked one of the twenty-eight students. "Irene?"

She stood and said, 'Then, First Lady, McClintock called African American criminals 'super-predators' that needed to be brought to their heels. And they were in the form of the Violent Crime Control and Law Enforcement Act of 1994, sharpening a federal sentencing scheme that forced judges to hand-down mandatory sentences for crimes that targeted criminal acts primarily committed in urban communities and essentially by Latinos and African-Americans."

"I couldn't have put that any more eloquent," Naim said, smiling. "Thank you. Any questions before we continue? I'm going to have a few of your present your sentencing strategies from the podium. We're going to ascertain how you grow over the course of the semester."

A lone hand was raised. Naim consulted the seating chart, and said, "Jake?" He pointed at the gold-haired, green-eyed, Jake Franta like the President shooting on index fingers at a member of the White House press Corp in the Rose Garden during a press conference.

"Why'd you request we dress in courtroom attire?" Jake asked, raising a skeptical eyebrow. "And do we have to for every class this semester?"

"Great questions. I wanted you all to get a feel for getting up early and racing off to an early morning courtroom appearance. Dressed and ready to perform," Naim said, pacing across the stage. "This is only today, for now. I will ask again twice more. Once with advance notice and once without to prepare you for an emergency in-chambers appearance. I will e-mail you between three and six a.m. the day I'd like you dressed for an emergency. And expect a surprise. Jake, I'd like you to come up and present your sentencing position for your client." Jake stood and made his way to the stage, and then Naim said, "Class, I'd like you to take notes identifying the good and bad of his argument. Please do nitpick with regard to his delivery, word choice, and any other factor. Especially his ability to tell a story."

And Naim was off. His first day working towards molding young men and women into fine attorneys had commenced. His efforts wouldn't make the news, but undoubtedly, some prosecutor across America would loathe the criminal-defense-chimeras he set out to create.

CHAPTER 4

9:45 a.m.

Georgetown, Washington D.C.—Residence of Percy Weston

Mere coincidence brought David Thurman into a ritzy, small area of D.C. at the same time as the stranger. He and his father, Carson Thurman, moved into a Tudor-style home adjacent to a church with his father's latest bimbo, a bust-heavy college professor named, Connie, who drank too much beer and loved sports. The stranger came to Georgetown three days later, settling into the cottage on the property of the area's only Mormon church.

Thurman was bored with life that spring—when Connie and his father weren't making rambunctious love with her belting out cringe-worthy pleas to God, they were spending his alimony catering to Connie's physical beauty and taking walks along the nearby Potomac River—so he used his time learning all about the stranger residing on the grounds of the church. Thurman had decided his first act was to surveil. Watch the man's every move. Because Thurman was ten-years-old and the only child of divorcees, he was well-trained in the art of watching adults. Investigating and observing them. To begin with, like any surveillance, he needed a watch station. No place better than his bedroom window; it had an unrivaled view over-looking the stranger's cottage. In his father's army duffel he found a pair of modern binoculars, and at the Georgetown University school store, he stole a composition book and pack of ballpoint pens to log the movement of his target. His first misdemeanor for which he wasn't arrested.

The first thing Thurman noticed was the stranger kept odd hours. He cleaned the church grounds during the day. By seven p.m. he left the cottage with a book bag, riding a bicycle, the same one that he had come to town on. He was a man that kept a strict schedule. Punctual. A man of great repetition.

Three months into Thurman's investigation the stranger's cottage was raided by Metropolitan P.D. He was accused of peddling cocaine and reefer on the Georgetown U campus. Later that night, Thurman stole one of his father's guns and hid it under his pillow. He feared the stranger had caught him surveilling his moves and thought that he reported them to the authorities, bringing about his arrest. Bored even more thanks to his subject's arrest, though, Thurman ratcheted up his mischievousness. He was caught swiping a camcorder from an electronics shop on the area's main shopping track. Connie conspired with his father and sentenced him to two weeks of solitary confinement in his bedroom.

Perfect.

Not a problem for Thurman who used the binoculars to spy on the church's pastor. He watched the pastor welcome a new stranger to reside in the cottage, who kept up the same routine as the last arrested resident. To Thurman's fresh detective-eye the new stranger looked a lot like a drug pusher. Verification arrived when the stranger was escorted to a police cruiser followed by a handcuffed, Pastor Jonathan McKee. Thurman knew it. It was the moment he began to believe in coincidence.

That was thirty-six years ago.

Today, forty-six-year-old, David Thurman, dressed in a long-sleeved T-shirt and cotton sweatpants—both with Georgetown University embellishments—jogged up to an elegant Tudor house in Georgetown, Washington, D.C. A two-man diplomatic security detail was posted at the front of the white-painted house. *What about the back, brainiacs?* Thurman thought. He felt sorry for the men who babysat, United States Supreme Court Chief Judge Percy Weston, a white-haired liberal appointed by former president Cotter. Their black Yukon Denali was parked between two orange cones in front of Justice Weston's purlieu, at the ready to whisk the judge wherever he wanted to go 24/7. Thurman estimated the rent-a-cops weren't necessary and another waste of taxpayer's dollars. The biggest problem in Georgetown—where the murder rate was negative some-odd percentage points—was drunkard Georgetown students walking pass the judge's home from an off-campus party. Occasionally, they taunted the judge's security. Tired their patience. Gave them a little excitement. Most times they were ushered along, but there was a time or two a student found their faces pushed into the judge's lawn with guns in their faces.

Having a bonafide security team in Washington was reserved for the real players—the president and Vice President, no doubt, the Secretary of State, Secretary of Defense, Director of the FBI, and the Director of the CIA. All other players were left to fend for themselves unless, like Justice Weston, a specific threat was made to take their lives. Thurman knew that Justice Weston had a credible threat on his life, because he had made it on an Internet message board used by ISIS sympathizers. The site was religiously monitored by the CIA.

Both bodyguards had red hair and freckles. Strawberry Shortcake's brothers, no? One had more hair than the other. When Thurman slowed in front of them and jogged in place, they pushed their blazers back, setting their hands on their pistols. *Perhaps, I should have called ahead,* but he wanted to surprise the justice.

"Guys," Thurman said politely. *God, I hate political correctness. It's loaded with lies and deceit.* "I'd like to have a brief word with Justice Weston. Think you can give him a ring and ask him to come out?"

The men gave Thurman a menacing stare, and one of them said, "Absolutely…not?"

The way the men looked at each other screamed that they had no idea who they denied an unscheduled face-to-face with the judge.

"Why don't you run along," the one with the shorter hair said. He was irritated by the request.

Thurman shook his head and thought. *How could it be that these imbeciles not respect my presence?* "I won't be, as you say *running along* until one of you at least advise the justice of my request."

Neither bodyguard replied. They stared at the man before them with an uncertain glare and wondered what kind of simpleton jogged to the front of the chief justice's home and demanded a meeting. The number one judge in the world.

Again, the one who was losing the hairline war spoke. "I'm going to ask you to keep it moving or I'll have you arrested for trespassing."

Thurman snickered.

"You're a real piece of work," he said, smiling condescendingly. He was extremely pissed that some D.C. rent-a-suit had the gall to attempt to block his access to Justice Weston.

"My work is to protect the justice, period. If I was to call him about a jogger's request for him to appear I wouldn't be worth a damn to this great country, would I?" the guard with the longer red hair said, smirking.

In one swift violent motion, Thurman put a neat hole the size of a nickel between the tough SOB's eyes. Punishment for his grandiose insolence. Then, he sent a silence shot slicing through the partner's scalp. "I don't think either of you are worth a damn to this country or apparently to the good judge," Thurman said, confiscating the dead men's side arms. "Thank you, kindly. Just exercising my right to bear arms, fellas," he said, walking up the narrow path towards Judge Weston's front door. He whistled the Alfred Hitchcock Psycho score and thought, *á bon chat, bon rat*. To a good cat, a good rat.

Ready or not, here I come.

CHAPTER 5

New York, NY—*New York Times* Headquarters

Brandy Scott settled behind a glass desk inside of her well-appointed office at the *New York Times* headquarters. She wasn't senior enough to have an office facing the New York skyline, but she had a helluva view of the Hudson River overlooking New Jersey. The Statue of Liberty's torch burned prismatically, paying homage to her freedom of speech, the Amendment to the Constitution she valued most. She'd been a stellar political editor with the newspaper giant for several years and the office, albeit a small one, applauded her profit-making articles.

Her desktop computer was powered on. She struck a key to bring it back to life and stared at the first draft of a story that promised to cut into political programming. BREAKING NEWS. The editor had returned from reporter, Joshua Cooperman's cubicle, having grilled him for confirmation on a source's account of the marital separation of New York mayor, Bob Rodin, and his wife. Apparently—Johanna Rodin—had text pictures of her recent bob-job (rumored to had been paid for on the taxpayer's dime) to New York Giants, veteran running-back, Bryant Jackson, with the message: *Wait 'till you get a taste of these.* She included a smiley face with the tongue out.

Brandy was elated about the article's potential. A new piece to smear the mayor's office, actively engaged in campaigning for the Democratic presidential nominee, James MacDonald, who the polls had in a dead heat with Republican nominee, Donna Lincoln. Despite the newspaper's reputation of having a left-wing slant, she was a staunch republican that bent her articles to the right, as clandestinely as possible.

On her desk was a loving snapshot in a crystal frame of her with her beau on a trip to San Francisco at the Golden Gate Bridge. She glanced at the time on the computer screen, and then, realized that he was out of class and a call from her was warranted.

He answered on the second ring. "Good morning, Dr. Naim Butler. I so love the sound of that."

"I reckon, I do also beautiful. How're you this morning?" he asked with a bright grin on his face. "I'm great. How was your first day in front of a classroom?"

"Still can't believe it. And it's hardly a classroom. It's a damn lecture hall with over a hundred seats. There are twenty-eight students enrolled in the class."

"Twenty-eight lucky brats," she said, chuckling. "I miss you."

"It's been three days since we've seen each other. But who's counting?"

"I am, so, dinner tonight to celebrate. I'll pick you up at seven."

"What're you doing here?" he said.

"Excuse me."

"Pardon me, Brandy," he said, adding, "Marco's mother just barged into my office."

"Oh my," Brandy said, chuckling sarcastically. "So much for a bright day."

"Trust me, that hasn't changed one bite, babe. I'll see you tonight, hun bun."

He blew her a kiss through the phone before hanging up.

Brandy stared at a painting on her office wall, wishing Sinia crawled into a hole, and hibernated for the rest of her life. She didn't hate the woman because she loved Marco and knew that he needed his mother. And she was confident that Naim was a faithful and didn't romantically desire, Sinia Love. Nevertheless, she wished the woman went home to North Carolina and stayed there. Brandy e-mail alert chimed, snapping her out of her ferocious reverie. She grabbed her computer mouse and pulled up her e-mail inbox. She had one new e-mail with the subject line: Exclusive Photos Do Not Share.

Clicking the first of five attachments, a photograph slowly appeared onto the screen. She recoiled in distaste. Each image was more heinous and demented than the last. Her heart raced uncontrollably as she picked up her desk phone and called her superior. The woman answered, and without preamble, Brandy said, "I just forwarded you an exclusive e-mail. Justice Percy Weston has been savagely slain decapitated and castrated.

"Delightful," Quinn Berkeley said cheerfully, looking forward to the story being the topic on that night's dinner tables. Thanks to the Times.

CHAPTER 6

10:35 a.m.

New York, NY—Columbia University

Columbia University had been, Marco knew, the crème de la crème. He adored the old buildings, welcomed the pricey tuition, and understood the huge number of campus police and cameras.

For some odd reason, to him anyways, students tried hard to mix with Morningside Heights—typical rich Upper West Side neighborhood —residents. He was there for an Ivy League education and any community efforts would be made in black and brown communities that truly needed his skill set. *All grown up*, he thought, walking pass a bronzed statue of a naked gentleman just sitting there apparently thinking. He was in the school's main plaza and copped a squat in front of Low Memorial Library to pass the time away before his first class: Academic Writing & Critical Reading. Just a young man thinking about a bright future. A future with a resume that listed his undergrad studies at the university attended by the first black President of the United States. *Not bad*, he thought, considering I've only known my dad nine months and turned out quite well. Although his mother had lied to him about who his father was, she was partly responsible for his academic adeptness. The other part was inherited from Naim Butler. Since his move from North Carolina, back in January, he'd fully embraced the New York City culture, and the father he loved like he had known him his entire life. "So blessed," he said aloud, but quietly. He faded into a daydream but was roused to reality by the soft touch of Amber's hand to his sweaty neck. He lightly jerked causing her to smile.

"You were really off in space," she said, staring at him. "You didn't even see me approaching." Her romantic, tawny eyes flirted with him.

He stood, hugged her and said, "Your eyes become more brownish with the sun shining on them." His NBA forward-esque physique swallowed her svelte, ballerina frame. "I was just thinking about how far I've come as a New Yorker." Pulling her closer, he said, "And how devoted I've been to making you the happiest woman alive."

"Look at you. All charm this morning," she said, smiling.

"Every morning." He raised a bushy eyebrow mirroring his father's, causing her to burst into laughter. Marco's demeanor demonstrated an absurd level of confidence. And he was thankful for his superior qualities.

He was equally thankful for the things shaping his future: his major (political science); his job (sales associate at 59th & Lexington Bloomingdale's); her major (English); and her job (sales associate at the Fifth Avenue Apple Store). They had been building a committed relationship for eight months, after meeting at their prestigious Manhattan prep school, Clive Davis Hall.

"Yes, every morning, big head," she said, grabbing his hand. "We better get to class."

Nineteen-year-old, Amber King, was born and raised in Newark, New Jersey currently resided Alpine, New Jersey—once deemed America's richest zip code and home to dozens of celebrities—with her father (an obstetrician) and mother (a Wall Street broker). Today her luxuriant hair rested on her shoulders, framing an oval-shaped face, housing dark-brown eyes, slim nose, and voluptuous lips. She was enveloped in a creamy almond-complexion, tall and strutted down the streets gracefully like a catwalk destroyer.

The campus had a Monday-morning feel to it. Most of the students were bustling about getting the semester underway. In that light, Marco had a feeling of optimism that he desired to savor, and he was unapologetically grateful.

Taking her laptop bag in his hand, he began to escort her to the only class that they scheduled to take together.

"Have you talked to your dad about his class, yet?" she asked genuinely. She had a high level of respect for Naim—he future father-in-law.

"No, but I did text him. I had two dozen roses and a card sent to him, also."

Then a boom sound pierced the air in the distance.

"You hear that?"

A loud, rapid cracking followed a gunshot report; sound traveling quicker than the spray of bullets. The speed said the shots were nearby, seemingly from somewhere right inside of the school's quad.

"Shooter," said Marco, squeezing Amber's hand tighter and pulling her, quickly but not panicked, towards the Thinking Man statue. Gunshots on a college campus meant crazed lunatic. Or terrorist. There had been a lot of homegrown insanity in the United States over the past few years. Violent mass murderers. He feared he was in the crosshairs of an attack, rushing to take cover.

Two of the bullets hit the statue, spraying marble, but a third one hit Marco Butler squarely in the right shoulder. It made him spin, leaving behind a twirl of blood. The bullet penetrated and exited cleanly, ripping flesh and muscle but missed the heart and the lungs.

Not too much blood, no bones fragments.

CHAPTER 7

10:35 a.m.

New York, NY—74th Street and 5th Avenue Residence of Naim Butler

In a pencil skirt and blouse, strategically unbuttoned, cleverly exposing tanned cleavage, Sinia parked on the edge of Naim's mahogany desk. "Tables are for asses…you know the rest," he said blinking, shaking his head and smiling. They were in Naim's sophisticated home office and the tension was thick. He folded his hands and placed them on the desk in front of a wireless keyboard. Pulling off his glasses he said, "Despite my instructions you're here. Unannounced." He leaned his head to the side, chastising her with his bold eyes.

"Ginger, sent me in. I mean, I am the mother of your only begotten son. At least she recognizes and respects that," she said seductively un-crossing and re-crossing her smooth, long legs.

He imagined her whipping out a cigarette, lighting it, taking a long puff, and then blowing rings of smoke in his face. Homage to a seventies call girl.

Naim Butler's office was painted baby-blue with high navy-blue colored ceilings. Two chandeliers lit up the room along with antique sconces. Behind his custom-made six-feet mahogany desk, he sat in an expensive executive chair. Diplomas decorated the wall behind him.

"Are you implying that I don't respect you?" he asked, standing. He walked to a vintage credenza and snatched a pastry from a silver tray on top of it. He took a bite and finished chewing, before asking, "Crème brûlée? I had them delivered this morning from the baker."

"Flowers from the boo, Brandy?" she asked, ignoring his offer. She ripped a petal from one of the roses, poking out of the arrangement on his desk.

He grinned, plucked the card from the bouquet and passed it to her. He took another bite of his dessert. "We have a great son, huh? The one thing you've blessed me with. See, because I am teaching him valuable things early, he sent his father's congratulatory flowers." He sat on a Chesterfield sofa across the gargantuan office. *Far enough away*, he thought. "Why are you here?"

"The Feds took forty thousand dollars cash from me," she replied deadpan.

"Then, you should be at their office."

"They implied that I could be trafficking cash. Little ole me," she said, pouting.

"Doesn't sound criminal to me," he said and heard his cell phone buzz. He ignored it.

"My point exactly," she said, standing. She walked to where he was, sat on the over-sized arm of the sofa, allowing her elbow the rest on his broad shoulder for balance.

He chuckled. "Sinia, why are you here?"

Staring out of the floor-to-ceiling window, she sat silently before falling gently into his lap. Her derriere landed perfectly on his pelvis. She snuggled her head on his shoulder, tossing an arm around his neck.

Naim kept his hands pressed on the sofa. His palms were wet from sweat and he felt his neck becoming moist with Sinia's tears.

"Why are you doing this?" he asked tenderly, keeping his hands to himself. He wasn't falling for any of her womanly traps.

"I really need you and you treat me so coldly. Like trash," she cooed, raising her head, looking into his eyes. His cell phone buzzed, he ignored it again. The sight of her tears forced him to unearth courage reserved for physical threats. There was no way he'd allow her tears to convince him to say goodbye to his fidelity to Brandy Scott. Returning her deep stare, he said, "I simply asked why were you here. It's a fair question, Sinia." He knew how powerful it was to call a woman by their name during a conflict.

"Do you realized how rude that is? Your delivery is horrific."

Do you realize it was your boyfriend that tried to kill me? he thought, but lacked the bravery to tell her that. "Sinia," he said gingerly, "the government took money from you. Why?"

"You're still dismissing me, but I'm going to get to the point, because I know I'm not really wanted here."

Now we're getting somewhere. You're not.

She glanced at the floor. "I arrived at JFK two days ago with the cash to give to Marco. Homeland Security searched my carry-on bag, found the money, and confiscated it."

"They didn't say why?"

"Vaguely. Claimed I was stopped because I booked the flight hours before takeoff and didn't check any bags."

"That's bullshit. You don't look like an Arabic woman to me," he said, realizing how racist and discriminatory his comment could be interpreted.

"Tell me about it."

"So…" he began and then fell into a silent stupor.

"So, I need you to get *our* son's money back," she said, looking at him again.

"Where'd the money come from?" he asked with a hint of suspicion.

She caught the shade dripping from the question. "Drug sales," she replied, smirking condescendingly. "Some of it was pulled out of the bank last week. Some were from my home safe."

"All legal?"

"You're an ass."

"I'm asking questions as an attorney, not your friend."

"Of course, it's all legal," she said, kissing his lips. "This doesn't have to be so formal." she wiggled on his lap, looking to arouse him.

Ignoring her advance, he said, "OK, I will look into it. I need the bank withdrawal receipt of bank statement to prove the legitimacy of the funds. For them, not me. And the contact information of the people responsible."

"It'll get the statement printed from online banking," she said, running a finger down his chest. "You don't love me anymore?" she asked over the sound of an unceasing knock on the door before it opened.

"Sorry to interrupt," Ginger said frantically.

Naim pushed Sinia from his lap. *Why the hell did have her on my lap for so long?* "What is it, Ginger?"

"It's Marco, sir. He's at the Columbia University Hospital. Amber tried reaching you by phone twice already before she called the office line."

Naim was grabbing his car keys before he asked, "Did she say what happened?"

"Oh my God," Sinia said, fixing her clothing.

"He's been shot." She watched her boss freeze. He was usually in command of his emotions, but she witnesses him internally losing it. "It's all over the news."

CHAPTER 8

New York, NY—Columba University Hospital

Naim Butler backed away from the hospital room windows and the media hounds converging on Columbia University Hospital on the streets below. He felt like a failure. Regret burned in the depths of his soul. His life was last. He should have hired a security team to protect his son.

Paperwork was being written to have Marco released and Naim wanted to go up rather than down to leave. The last thing he wanted was to be accosted by reporters. Obviously going up was a dead end, stopping at the roof. The only advantage to being on the roof was that he could jump off of it, paying for his screw up.

The alternative, going straight down and fighting his way through them. That was tantamount to walking into a swarm of lions: he was sure they'd eat him alive. Running wasn't an option really, nor was suicide.

A nurse rolled Marco back into the room. Naim smiled at his brave son. He watched Amber rush to his side and felt a deep sense of love between them. He longed for Brandy Scott. Sinia remained by Naim's side as if they were a happy family.

They weren't.

"Can somebody tell me about the idiot that shot me?" Marco asked, pushing a button on the side of the bed. He was quite nonchalant for being a shot teen. When he was upright his face scanned all of the supporters by his side.

"Oh, that's an easy one," Naim said. "He's dead. Campus police shot him. Nineteen times." He raised an eyebrow and smiled. "Overkill."

"Don't worry about that," Sinia said, walking to his bedside. She ran a loving hand along his cheek, frowning at the sling that restricted his left arm. The bullet had torn tendons in his shoulder for which shoulder surgery repaired. "We have to get you back to Raleigh today so that you can rest up without the maddening press outside."

"Absolutely not going to happen," Naim said matter-of-factly.

Sinia cut her eyes at him. They screamed for him to shut-the-hell-up.

"Mom...dad," Marco said, watching the doctor enter the room. "I'm fine. No need to relocate me, mom. I live in New York. Please get used to that. I can deal with the media." He turned to the doctor and said, "Doc, can you confirm, please?"

"Sounds like a family affair to me, but you're visibly capable of handling the media," the doctor replied, smiling at his young, eloquent patient. "Medically, I can say that this was a clean flesh wound and it'll heal up quite fine. There will be a small scar when we remove the stitches. I'm going to prescribe a painkiller and suggest that you rest a few days."

"Doc, I hear all of that, but rest really isn't an option," Marco said in a friendly, but stern tone. "As you know fall classes began today and I'm not going to fall behind."

"Listen to the doctor," Amber suggested. "There will likely be another week off. There's ten other wounded students and three dead."

"Five," said the doctor. "We lost two more less than an hour ago. Marco is the only one not in critical condition and able to leave today."

"Wow," Naim said. "Blessed."

"My ass it is. This city is horrible and dangerous,"—Sinia said, causing every eye to whip in her direction— "and you're coming back to North Carolina. Today. You should've just went to Duke." She threw her back into a wall. A miniature meltdown.

Naim scoffed sarcastically.

"Nothing is going to happen, mom," Marco said. "I will relax, or rest, as the good doctor put it, but I will support the deceased families by attending funerals and I will go to classes when they start. With or without this sling. I will not allow anyone to block my education or force me to live in fear. Not going to happen, mom."

"Spoken like a true Butler," said Naim. "Daddy's little man."

After a brief silence and Sinia picking her chin up from the floor, Naim said, "The prince has spoken." He grinned from ear-to-ear, antagonizing Sinia. "Now, let's get you out of here and home."

Naim looked out the window. The number of reporters had doubled. To the doctor, he asked, "Is there a service elevator and does it lead to the parking garage?" His adrenaline for survival kicked in and he had a plan.

———

Naim had been exposed to a few life-or-death battles and escaping an area hospital with aggressive reporters looking to pounce on him was one. His life had had many highs, but his mind was concentrated on the lows as he pressed the down button outside of the elevators used for orderlies to transport food and bedridden patients that needed to be kept out of the public's eye.

The elevator door opened, everyone boarded and Naim pressed "G" for the garage. There were signs on board that ordered him and his clam to keep all patients data confidential and to wash their hands often to avoid the spread of germs. A woman smiled at them from a poster promoting the Labor Day breast cancer awareness walk to raise money for research. *A noble cause*, Naim thought, vowing to make a financial contribution as soon as the dust settled. The elevator jerked once, and the car darkened and stopped between floors—trapped. A scenario mirroring death, but then moments later the elevator shook and continued down to the garage level.

The door buzzed, lurched open finally, Naim and crew exited and scanned the area for his armored Cadillac Escalade. They also looked for reporters. There were none, but bare mattresses were leaning against a wall like supermarket carts under the open end of a wall shoot. *Primitive*, Naim thought.

Everyone hopped into the truck, Naim started it and looked at Marco in the passenger's seat.

Naim said, "It's quiet now, but I assure you the moment we exit this garage we will be surrounded by the media."

"Sounds like New York SWAT," Sinia said, shooting at the City That Never Sleeps.

"You know," Naim said, looking back at her. "Keep it up and in the trunk you go. Your visual isn't helpful at all."

"Screw you," she replied, rolling her eyes.

"Been there, done that," he said, turning his head towards his son. "Do you have your statement up and ready to go?"

"I do and it's partially memorized," Marco replied, looking at the statement on his cell phone.

"Good. Do not deviate from the message. Maintain eye contact with cameras. And do not say 'um'," Naim admonished.

"What do I look like Donna Lincoln?" Marco asked, laughing.

"No, she's a woman and running for president of the free world. You're a shot college student," he replied, chuckling, trying to lighten the tension trapped in the car.

CHAPTER 9

New York, NY—*New York Times* Headquarters

Glued to her chair, stone-faced, thinking about a cigarette—a habit she'd kicked ages ago—Brandy Scott was watching CNN on a television, the BBC on a laptop, and the local NBC news-affiliate on an iPad. She was heavily interested in what correspondents had to say. They knew she surmised, next to nothing at this point about the campus shooting, and the justice's death hadn't been on their radar. Was she the only person other than the killer that knew about Judge Percy Weston's death? She knew that she could put her exclusive intelligence on the tips of their tongues with a five-minute phone call. But she'd wait. She wanted to hear from the campus shooting victims, the people who had seen the bloodshed wanted to know: Was the campus shooting and the judges' murder carried out by the same person or group?

An Israeli girl, interviewed on CNN, describe the loud blast that preceded the gunfire: "There was a caravan. I can't be sure of the make and model. It slammed into a tree and seconds after the driver got out." She paused, holding back tears. "It blew up. The shooter started killing people seconds later."

Brandy used the TV remote to mute CNN and turned up the volume on the BBC. A British student and part-time UBER driver described the killer: black male, dark skin, dreadlocks, handsome, all-American. But the Uber driver didn't see much else because after the shooter's car exploded the driver took cover under the dashboard of his Jaguar until the bullets stopped.

Minimizing the Internet browser, Brandy pulled up a notebook app and stared at the blank screen before typing a single word.

Dreadlocks.

She used the app because all of the recorded "notes" simultaneously loaded to related apps on her iPhone and iPad, giving her access to them across her Apple devices. Brandy's eyes returned to the TV screen as a nicely dressed reporter stood in front of the LIVE camera feed next to an attractive young man, Marco Butler, recounting some of the facts for the correspondent. In the background was Sinia Love with her hand on the elbow of Naim Butler. She looked at the sight painfully. Not because Naim appeared to comfort Marco's mother, but the sight of the freshman's arm in a sling worried her.

Marco described hearing a loud bang before an explosion. In an attempt to protect his high school sweetheart he tried taking cover behind Thinking Man before he pushed her to the ground, but not in time to avoid being shot in the shoulder. He did not see the heartless monster because he hit the deck to continue being armor for Amber. When the first round of bullets stopped, the couple ran to Amsterdam

Avenue. They flagged a pedestrian who whisked them to Columbia University Medical Center.

"Could someone assume this is the universe's retribution for the murder you committed earlier this year?" A reporter yelled at Marco.

Holy shit, Brandy thought. Her mood shifted further down to the pain zone. *What kind of animal asks an eighteen-year old that?*

She watched Naim step fully into the frame. He stood tall and protective next to his son. "Whoa..whoa," he said, throwing his eyes into the air, apparently in deep thought. Carefully crafting his word, she figured. He added, "My son was shot on his first day of college, that is, and will be the only discussion being held today. Or tomorrow, in fact." Flames escaped his forehead.

"But," the reporters said, "if not for your best friend being a prosecutor he'd be in jail, as I said, for *murder*. Not at his first day of college." He paused, and then said, "As far as New Yorkers are concerned perhaps this was payback costing several other people their lives."

"You know." Naim said, chuckling. "This is laughable—"

"Dad," Marco interjected, cutting his father off before he dirtied the water. To the reporter, he said, "I was cleared of murder charges by the Manhattan DA's office, not my father's best friend who is a U.S. Attorney. It'll be wise if you acquire knowledge of the judicial process basics before insulting my father. And as of this moment, you're blacklisted. And by you, I mean the entire network. Columbia encourages students to stand for something. I guess my first act will be a petition blocking your reporters from being on campus inquiring about the shooting. Now I see why the Republican presidential nominee always regards the media as dishonest. And fake news. Good day."

Brandy smiled. She watched Marco and company scram as the reporter recovered by pivoting into a commercial. She picked up her cell phone and sent Naim a text message to contact her at his convenience.

Awaiting a reply, the network was back from a commercial break with a reporter in front of a white home. The banner on the bottom of the screen read: **Home of Chief U.S. Supreme Court Justice Percy Weston**. She looked at her computer screen and typed another word:

Showtime!

They had the story, but she had the smoking photos.

CHAPTER 10

Southeast, Washington, D.C.

David Thurman's feet felt heavy, pacing through the sparsely decorated and furnished efficiency in a dingy apartment complex on the Southeast side of D.C. He forced himself to watch the boring local news, switching between that and the trivial political cable news networks. He patiently waited for his doctoring of the judge's features to be aired, preceded by a BREAKING NEWS banner. Despite his bravado and an OCD-driven desire for neatness and cleanliness, he put it aside to remain in character by using the derelict building as a command center. His rendezvous point. He did a good job assuring the building's tenants —especially the drug dealing thugs that crowded the stoop—didn't get a whiff of his purpose for invading the capital. Just the night before he had heard a hail of bullets, rumored to be a failed drug stash house robbery attempt. The fevered pitch of the bullets forced him to feel right at home. Despite the filthiness. Back on the battlefield.

Thurman suddenly felt dizzy. His heart rate quickened and his vision became cloudy.

"This is CNN breaking news." He heard the news anchor announce before a snazzy photo of Chief Justice Percy Weston appeared in a small box at the top of the screen.

Watching an MPD spokesperson on the screen fielding questions from reporters allowed a nervous smile to spread across Thurman's face. There was no way the assassin could avoid the ensuing investigation. *The hunter would become the hunted*, he thought. *Finally my will, will be done. I just tipped the scales of justice on my terms, and there isn't much to be done about it. Well, besides planning a funeral.*

When the messenger was through expressing how the investigation was on-going, he exposed how the death of Percy opened an appointment to the bench by the next president. He finished the report with exciting news for Thurman—his intended effect. "This could be another deciding factor for voters. But, first, we have more on the campus shooting in New York City at Columbia U."

Twenty minutes later, Thurman decided to celebrate. To feed his addiction, he found himself on the stoop of his building, buying PCP from one of the dealers. That was the sole reason, he was able to ignore the poor condition of his apartment. That and it was the perfect cover. Every law enforcement agency no doubt looked for him to leave the DMV, but he stayed right under their noses. He was dressed in dirty coveralls and a sad fedora—an out of place white man in the ghetto. The neighbors allowed him there because he bought drugs from them. He was a handsome payday that they would protect. Sadly, neither of them had regard for the undercover agents that surveilled the area in an effort to take down local drug rings.

CHAPTER 11

Georgetown, Washington, D.C.—1583 Twenty-Eight Street, NW
Residence of Percy Weston

After a sadistic killer sucker-punched Georgetown and moseyed away, leaving a vacuum of death, panic, and confusion, the lesson of the day seemed clear if you were in law enforcement. At first blush, the Columbia U story seemed like a big deal, but the murder of Chief Justice Percy Weston was hailed universally as a *bombshell*. Reporters from the East Coast to the West Coast were hyperventilating about the significance of each blockbuster. DC MPD Detective Suzanne McGee imagined TV new producers in their war rooms crafting a nickname for the crimes with a "-gate" suffix.

Detective McGee. Single, white, green-eyes, long blonde hair—accurately described her visible attributes. Wearing push-up bras to enhance her cleavage and sporting expensive high-heels to crime scenes encouraged people to view her as incompetent. All beauty and no brains. They'd be ignoring her fifteen-years in law enforcement, five-years starring as the lead TV detective in the Emmy award-winning series, The Westwood Beat, and undoubtedly wrong. By rotation, McGee assumed the role of lead detective in the investigation of the dead judge.

"Look at this shit," Detective McGee said to her partner, pulling up to Judge Weston's street in their government-issued Chevrolet Impala. "All hands on deck."

Police, ambulances, CSI, coroner, and Federal conveyances were stationed strategically, blocking traffic from entering or exiting Twenty-eighth Street, NW without permission.

"They're not happy to see the Babes of DC policing show up," Detective Bald Eagle said, looking at two MPD officers whispering and pointing at the Impala.

Detective Marissa Bald Eagle. Champion dancer—ballroom and tap —war hero, suicidal. Detective Bald Eagle took up dangerous demonstrations against sanity having tried skydiving, race car driving and had someone shoot at an apple on her head. While chasing death she came across success as a sharpshooter in the US Army. Raised on the Lakota reservation in South Dakota, she left to join the military on a quest to defend the United States, ultimately defending Native Americans. When not solving crimes she was a glam-mom to a nine-year-old daughter, who lived with her ex-husband and his new wife.

"Sucks to be them," Detective McGee said, shutting down the car. She pulled down the visor, looked in the mirror, and smiled. She touched up her pink lipstick, tucked auburn hair behind her ear, and then popped an Altoid into her pouty mouth.

Detective Bald Eagle was leering at the four-bedroom Tudor—its manicured, expansive lawn decorated with two dead men in black suits. CSI staff patrolled the grounds looking for clues and forensics to lead to the killer or killers. In the distance was the dome of a gazebo in the back of the house. The opened garage door revealed matching Mercedes S-class sedans. Outside of the garage in a short driveway was a third car, a blue Jaguar XFS.

"And action," Detective McGee said, opening her car door. She stepped out of the car, threw on gaudy Chanel sunglasses, and grabbed a three-by-five denim covered Versace notepad. Walking towards the crime scene, her partner in tow, she used an expensive pen to jot a question in her notepad: *Whose car is in the driveway?*

Approaching the crime scene tape, it was raised and veteran MPD Officer John Herr said, "Now that the stars have arrived, we can truly get this show on the road."

"Can it Herr," Detective Bald Eagle said fierily, furrowing a perfectly arched eyebrow. "Getting to business, I would assume there's a rather sophisticated video surveillance system, wouldn't you?"

"There is," Officer Herr said, accepting his admonition. "And already sent in a chain-of-custody pouch to HQ." He nodded, looking for their approval. He didn't get it. "Come on, let me show you what we've got."

CHAPTER 12

Georgetown, Washington, D.C.

Historic Georgetown was a thriving neighborhood, commercial, and entertainment district located in Northwest Washington, D.C. It was positioned along the Potomac River and founded in 1751. The port of Georgetown predates the city of Washington and the establishment of the federal district by forty years. In 1871, the United States Congress created a new consolidated government for the whole District of Columbia, and in 1895 an act was passed repeal Georgetown's remaining ordinances and renamed the neighborhood's streets to conform with those in the City of Washington.

Today the intersection of Wisconsin Avenue and M Streets serves as Georgetown's primary commercial corridor, containing high-end designer boutiques, bars, restaurants and the Georgetown Park Mall. Its newest edition was the Washington Harbor waterfront restaurants at K Street, between 30th and 31st.

Georgetown was home to the main campus of Georgetown University, and numerous other landmarks, like the Volta Bureau, and the Old Stone House, the oldest unchanged building in Washington. The embassies of France, Sweden, Venezuela, and others were there; but amidst all of this history and grandeur was the home of Chief Justice Weston.

Amongst the puzzled looky-loos cordoned off at the corner of Justice Weston's street, amid the confusion of arriving police, an impeccably dressed man stood in the crowd. He had been mentally recording their activity with the utmost importance. The man wore preppy spectacles, a striped tie and had a tobacco pipe dangling from his lips.

Watching the investigation get underway, he caught himself gawking at the females possessing striking beauty approach an officer who seemed in charge of maintaining the crime scene's prosecutorial integrity. The man had developed an infatuation for the detective with the deep-bronze complexion and long, auburn hair that reached her calves. Pulling out his cellular phone he took pictures of her. *I shall find you, my sweet*, he mused.

When he put the phone back into his pocket, he glanced down at his fingertips. They were blood-red. He tried to wipe them clean before his arrival to the scene, but they were dyed red.

He looked up and one of the onlookers, a silver-haired man wearing a fedora was eyeing him. To get the man's mind off of his fingernails, he asked, "What do you think happened? All this drama is very exciting."

"Your guess may be as good as mine, considering I got nothing."

"If I were to speculate," David Thurman said, motioning up the street toward the colorful alphabet-rich squad of authorities, "I'd guess a murder investigation is underway." He gave impressive nod, aware of his chances of being questioned by police, who no doubt was going to canvas the area for clues leading to the suspect. And I'll be right here to throw them off.

CHAPTER 13

Georgetown, Washington, D.C.—Residence of Percy Weston

Having identified the two dead suits as failed bodyguards, detectives McGee and Bald Eagle walked up the pathway leading to the house, while scanning everything around them. They scoped out entry and escape points.

"It's safe to assume they were shot with silenced weapons because dispatch didn't receive a 911 call until a car driving by saw them dead. And by the time MPD arrived no killer came running out, and the bodies inside were already done up. Quite balefully, might I add," Officer Herr said, throwing his eyes between the two detectives for a reaction. "As of this moment, the udge's wife is at Georgetown University Hospital."

"Alive?" Detective McGee asked, walking onto the huge front porch. She typically asked most of the questions.

"For now," he replied, skirting around a low-level CSI staffer dusting the doorway for prints.

"What happened to the wife?" Detective Bald Eagle asked although she normally didn't ask questions at the scene of the crime. A strange attribute for a seasoned detective.

Coincidentally, that was Judge Weston's style during Supreme Court hearings. He hadn't presented a single question to a defendant or plaintiff before the Court in over fifteen years. He didn't want to choreograph anyone's argument. That wasn't his job. When before the highest court in the land it was imperative that a party's position was full, thought out, and designed to procure a victory before entering the well of the court.

"The wife's top jaw was broken off of her skull and her cheekbone was broken into her top jaw," Officer Herr said, stopping on the porch.

"A dirty wound?" Detective McGee asked.

"You could take her top jaw and move it around separate from her skull. Only the skin, the mucous membranes of the inside of the mouth, and some muscle attachments were holding her top jaw to the rest of her face. I've assumed she was stomped in the mouth."

"Some monster," blurted Detective Bald Eagle.

Walking through the front door, Officer Herr waved his hand around the front door, then waved his hand around the home's foyer with a view of the breathtaking great room, lower-level entertainment space, chestnut-paneled library, and charming paintings. The detective's pumps clicked and clacked against the mahogany inlaid flooring.

"The artwork is beautiful," Detective Bald Eagle said, marveling at a Andy Warhol print.

"You like art?" Officer Herr asked, frowning. "Let's go upstairs for the real gallery pieces. The judge has been decorated with scars, gashes, broken bones. Colored in red. And bound in silver. Cuffs." They started up the stairs, and he added, "There's a third victim. Black male, mid-twenties. He's wearing the judge's bench robe. Nude underneath. Gavel wrapped tightly in one hand."

"Guess we know who owns the Jag."

"We do," Officer Herr said. "Dorian Jackson. And here he is," he added, pointing to a light-skinned man with close-cropped waves lying in the master bedroom doorway. "He appears to have been trying to escape."

Upon stepping over Jackson and entering the bedroom, they observed a large amount of blood on a king-sized mattress beneath the judge. The judge had something wrapped around his neck, and it was apparent from the blood on his clothing and the bleeding from his head that he had sustained a lot of head trauma. The judge's bedroom was a blend of several shades of brown and a splash of blood-red. Quite the autumn decor.

"This room is in complete disarray," Detective Bald Eagle said, peering at the upturned furniture and bloodstained surfaces.

"Any drugs found?" Detective McGee asked.

"Nope, but I smell the weed like you," the officer replied.

"I want officers to canvass the neighborhood," Detective McGee said. "I'd love to yield an eyewitness. Was the wife able to talk?"

"You're kidding, right? She was gravely injured. Her mouth was practically off her face. Attempts to ask her questions would have been fruitless."

"This is purely overkill. A crime of passion," Detective Bald Eagle said. "These two were bludgeoned and strangled. The wife hit almost like an afterthought."

"Appropriate observation," Officer Herr said. "I'm interested in determining what the relationship between the Weston's and Jackson was. Friends or lovers?"

"I'm thinking swingers," Detective Bald Eagles said. "This is DC and its that kinda town." Her call phone rang and she answered it.

"Another great observation," said Officer Herr. "We just have to figure out if the judge was nude and in cuffs before the killer arrived or did they force them to create this stage at gun or knife point?"

Detective Bald Eagle concluded her call and slipped her cell phone back into her pocket. Then, she gave her partner a conspicuous head nod. They convened in the hallway, Bald Eagle leaned in and whispered, "The *New York Times* just broke a story about Weston's murder online."

"Why the secrecy? I don't like being whispered too," Detective McGee asked with a raised eyebrow.

"It includes photos of the judge postmortem," she said, before adding, "Maybe you need to have someone whispering to you. It's been a while sweetie."

CHAPTER 14

New York, NY—Columbia University

CNN, CBS, NBC, Fox, and Univision broadcast vans were parked on Columbia's magnificent campus. In addition to national news correspondents, communication majors were scattered about, preparing to write award-worthy pieces. The stage was set for an FBI led press conference in the middle of the school's quad. FBI Agent Sean Duffy had been in front of reporters, spectators, as well as concerned students and staff of the school. The agent was a short, solid man and packed a big punch. He specialized in taking down violators of the U.S. Crimes Code. He was at a make-shift podium flanked by New York's top brass:

Mayor Bob Rodin (with his marital problems), Jack Toussant and Columbia University President, Janet Elkind.

"First, I'd like to offer the country's sincere condolences to all victims of this horrific crime, to everyone here on the campus, and in New York City.

He then covered intelligence known to the public from eye-witness accounts, including social media posts. Those were unsurprising developments, and the federal agent was there with the current details. "Chiefly, the suspect who appeared alone staggered a mini-van onto the campus and slammed into a tree. Seconds later it exploded, apparently from a dirty-bomb that was detonated by the suspect or an accomplice. That was quickly followed by the culprit open firing on students and passerby with a recovered Daniel Defense DDM4A1 semiautomatic Tactical Rifle. He had emptied two thirty-round magazines, carrying six more in his cargo pants pocket. He came with two hundred forty bullets ready to go. Straight savage. He was shot by a campus policeman seventeen times at 10:41 am and pronounced dead at the scene."

A reporter yelled, "Can you tell us his name and details about this man. Is he a terrorist?"

Agent Duffy took a deep breath and sighed. "Can I fucking talk? He's been identified as Vladimir Leon. A black male of Haitian descent. He was hired by Columbia University in 2006 as a bilingual Research Assistant in the Stroke Division of Columbia's Department of Neurology. As of right now, we don't know of any terrorist connection."

"Why would a staff of the school kill anyone? Especially on the campus?" a reporter screamed above other reporter's trying to get a question in.

"Let me defer to school president, Janet Elkind," Agent Duffy replied, moving aside.

Elkind stepped in front of the microphone, and said, "Thank you," looking at the agent. Her voice was husky and she had a low boyish haircut. "Mr. Leon complained that he was being bullied by other employees, his co-workers in the study, particularly because he was Haitian. He perceived that he was regarded differently by other employees, who were Dominican. Allegedly, the Dominican employees belittled Mr. Leon's Spanish speaking ability, made racial comments about black people being less intelligent, and comments within his earshot about the first black U.S. president. These occurrences were reported to management, under investigation, and he was told it would be taken care of. It seems that he took care of it himself to the detriment of the beloved victims." She was teary-eyed and losing her calm composer.

Undeterred reporters hurled additional questions but were met with the stiff hand of Agent Duffy. He gently put a hand on Elkind's shoulder, before he shuffled the president away from the microphone, and said, "This is a fluid investigation, and we have divulged all that we can at this time. We will brief you all again the moment we learn more." He started moving away from the mic with an arm around Elkind's shoulder.

"Does this have any connection to the murder of Chief Justice Weston in Washington?"

FBI Agent Duffy stopped, backed up to the microphone, looked deeply into the lenses of the camera, and said, "We're praying that these two atrocities aren't connected. That would be a catastrophe." He walked away, and thought, *if they are connected things would be problematic.*

Two Killers.

One day.

Another yelled, "Mayor Rodin, you didn't speak. Are you going to divorce your wife?"

The mayor's stoned expression confessed all, before he said, "No," and continued off the podium.

CHAPTER 15

Williamsburg, Brooklyn, NY—William Vale Hotel

Naim and Brandy had made themselves presentable and were at the hip West Light Bar on the 22nd floor inside of The William Vale Hotel in Williamsburg, Brooklyn. Electric-blue and mustard-yellow velvet chairs and a polished stone bar anchored the vast room, with a three hundred sixty degree view of Brooklyn, Manhattan, and Queens from twenty-two stories up. Beautiful.

He was in denimed jeans, black blazer, with a shirt and tie. She had changed out of her office costume and into a little black dress, extremely high heels, pearls around her neck, and carried a handbag as pricey as a Manhattan Penthouse. She held a martini glass in her hand and took a grateful gulp. They both glanced at her Cartier wristwatch.

"What can I say. Time is money," she said, smiling.

"Tell me about it. We've both had very long days," he said, continuing to make small talk. He was exhausted and wanted to be in bed. Preferably with her.

"It's always a long day at the Times," she replied. "Especially when you break a story with photos of a dead judge."

"I read your piece. Is it OK for you to publish these sorts of photos?"

She turned towards him as she answered. "That depends. I've verified the source, so…"

"Wait a minute. You've talked to Judge Weston's killer?"

"Twice. And the FBI thrice. In person. The FBI Cyber Unit was livid that I published the photos."

Naim concealed his amazement. "Sounds very exciting," he said, touching her hand.

"You're being kind," she said, enjoying his touch.

Was he making a pass at her? He was such a charming romantic and she knew that nothing he did was an accident.

"It's only exciting until a killer wants to meet."

"Absolutely not," he said, sipping *Veuve Clicquot*. "No way I'm letting you meet any person bold enough to kill the Chief Justice. Hell, I've seen news accounts exposing the murder of four people. The judge's wife has about three breaths left. No way can you meet him." His subtle concern shifted to a smile. "Not alone, anyway."

"You're very concerned," she said, grinning. She opened her handbag and extracted a folded piece of paper. She unfolded it and read from it: "These are the people he hinted at as next on his list: The President of the United States; The Vice President of the United States; the Secretary of State; two undersecretaries of State; the president's chief of staff, Todd Decker; one of his two deputies, Carmen Vargan; two U.S. Senators; and the Attorney General."

"Quite an impressive list of victims," Naim said, watching bites from chef Andrew Carmellini being placed on the table.

"Thank you," she said to the waiter. And then to Naim, she said, "All but the senators have considerable access to the Oval Office. Perhaps the killer does, too. And *victims* is your word, not mine. As you know some people are looking for a change in Washington."

"Hence, the reason the Justice was killed. Removing Weston gets rid of a liberal, allowing the president to appoint someone else."

"Exact-a-Mundo," she said, pointing at him with a fork—steak on the end of it. "Someone's been watching CNN. But the new appointee will have to pass the scratch and sniff test of the conservatively lead Senate."

"So how are we to meet this animal?"

"We?"

"Yes, we. Or *oui*, if you like it in French." He winked.

"There will be a demonstration by Americans for Sentencing Reform tomorrow on Capitol grounds. He asked me to be there and he'd find me."

"So, he knows what you look like?" A bit of fear had crept into his voice.

"Everyone does. My headshot is public and on every article I write."

"Good point." He remembered reading her bio and admiring her *New York Times* online headshot nine months ago when they'd met. He had saved her from being run over by a drunk driver.

"Enough about me," she said, watching the waiter place their fifth of seven courses in front of them. "How's Marco?"

"He's Marco. Superman. Adonis. The school sent out an e-mail blast indicating classes were canceled this week. There's a candlelight vigil on Friday to mourn the deaths."

"But is his arm good?"

"Yes."

"So sad we have people that can mentally choose to kill innocent people," she said, looking into the air. "Is he at the dorm or your home?"

"You know we finally finished converting the former maid quarters into his private apartment. He's there with Amber. She's a wonderful girl."

"Yeah, I can see them marrying, have sex, kids, and grow old together. In that order."

"Like you and I?"

"Hold it. I'm no one's old," she said despite being four years his senior. Her stunning sex appeal and brilliance were her most stimulating attributes. The ones that he adored about her. It was nice for him to date a woman that enjoyed museums, operas, and roller coasters, which were his faves.

"Neither am I old." He was laughing. "I was, however, implying that we'd grow old together."

"Oh, OK," she said, "cause you were about to get shot." She playfully made her hand into a gun and shot at him. "Pow."

"You're too much," he said with a wide grin on his face. His mood saddened. "I had it out with Sinia. She, once again, tried convincing Marco to move back to North Carolina. She did it right in front of Amber with zero fucks given to the girl's feelings. Or his for the matter."

"What'd he say?"

"No doubt, he refused. And, then, she was pissy tonight because I made clear that she couldn't stay at my home. I'm at a point where she's more nuisance than anything else and her constant attempt to put a wedge between Marco and me is getting old. I had Ginger get her a room at the Peninsula."

"Certainly, she can't complain about you putting her up there," Brandy said, giggling.

"This is not funny," he replied, laughing. His laugh settled into a weak grin.

"On a more serious note, thanks for the transparency. Things with her will get better, Naim. You're a good man and time has proven you to be a grandfather—"

"Whoa, grandfather? You know something I don't?" He knew that she and Amber had had a few play dates.

She laughed. "Let me rephrase, great father. Two words."

He wiped his forehead, and said, "Be careful with your words editor. I'm barely a father. And not looking to be a grandfather before fifty."

She leaned over, brushed her lips against his ear, whispering, "Did I tell you what a superior lover you are, too?"

He licked his upper lip, glancing at her with a critical eye.

Brandy blushed. Everything he did turned her on. She said, "Don't let anyone question who you are, or your worth. You've overcome odds that typically leaves young, AA men in a vat of despair and hopelessness. I'm not going to sit here and stroke your outlook on life, which is always bright…"

"Except when my Achilles heel comes to town," he said, cutting her off. "But, continue, your words are blaming and therapeutic."

"Although older than you, I'm not your counselor," she said, laughing. "Let's just get that straight. And I would not excoriate or character assassinated your baby mama."

"OK. OK," he submitted. He seductively raised an eyebrow, and asked, "What time are you flying out to D.C. Tomorrow?"

"Haven't decided, but I may be taking Amtrak. Why?" She had an idea but asked.

"Sleep with me."

"Don't ask me to do something. Make me do something."

———

Naim brought Brandy to her third climax and continued his ministration until she stopped climbing up the wall, before he pulled a few inches out of her by getting into the push-up position. She gasped and he re-entered her.

Laying on top of her, he let her breathing normalize. "Nothing like a late night workout."

She pulled his head up by gripping his ears. Staring into his eyes, she said, "Your cockiness is dangerous."

"What did you say about my cock?" he asked, contracting his stomach muscles, forcing his penis to jump inside of her.

She emoted and stared at him. His chiseled shoulders and defined biceps made her wetter. He rested his head between her soft breast, kissing each hardened nipple. They were in a luxuriant Yotel suite, setting Naim back three-hundred-bucks for the night.

Brandy Scott was worth every penny.

CHAPTER 16

Washington, D.C.—Four Seasons Hotel

Through the night David Thurman had seduced two women: a twenty-four-hour diner waitress and a United States Capitol policewoman. Both of them enjoyed PCP with him and had been told a different lie explaining why he was in D.C. To the waitress, he was an Italian beautician with an appointment to do hair in the WH. To the officer, he was an economist in town for a summit to combat government wasteful spending. He didn't add that offing the justice shaved a few dollars off of the budget even if temporarily. He had crafted unique memories for them both. They'd never forget his sexual prowess. He had choked the waitress to the point of her passing out as he brought himself to satisfaction. He gave the cop multiple orgasms, spelling the alphabet on her vagina with his tongue and a diamond necklace. They had sex all night until she had to leave for duty. She was unaware that she had left him with Betty Weston's stolen necklace about her throat. What a gift from a one-night stand.

Leaving the Georgetown Four Seasons, Thurman hopped on his bicycle and rode along Wisconsin Avenue towards the Potomac River— just a tourist out and about taking in the morning sun. With the Weston inquiry in full-swing, he had work to do and the Columbia U shooting sharing the headlines was a problem. No one was to share or over-shadow his shine. He had dreamt of killing the campus shooter a second time. *Time to ratchet up the stakes*, he thought. Changing identities and ID was a priority. He needed a few subtle appearance alterations also. He had to take the bike for a swim in the Potomac and pick up his escape vehicle-a dated Nissan Maxima from the thirty-one hundred block of "P" Street, NW. Afterward, he was headed back to his ghetto hideout in all its stinking, steaming, roach-infested glory.

But first he had to make a call. He needed to retain a lawyer: One, Naim Butler.

CHAPTER 17

TUESDAY

Naim showered and dressed in gray jeans, black mohair loafers without socks, white button-up and a blue tie. The hip professor. He packed a bag of essentials, then, after closer inspection, grabbed a garment bag and packed that too. He had no idea how long he'd be in D.C. and wanted to be prepared for about two weeks. Things had moved quickly. His thoughts were running in different directions. His first case, a demand actually was underway. *How is this going to play out*, he thought.

Boarding the elevator, he headed to the garage to store his luggage in his Mercedes and was greeted by Marco who was onboard.

His son was in pajama bottoms and no shirt, the sling prominently shown. Marco said, "Going somewhere, pater?"

"To Washington—for a few days. Maybe a week." *Perhaps even longer,* he thought.

"Just leaving me here with my crazy mom, huh?"

Naim smiled. "Not my intent. I've never even thought of that."

"You're slippin'."

"I've kinda taken on a case. A big one. The kind of case I was built to do. You assured me that you were mentally, OK, and I want to allow you to prove that by not being an overbearing dad."

"No, I don't need that. Mom did enough of that for the last eighteen years."

"Good, so I am going to D.C. to handle a case that will do exciting things for my future. And yours, too."

"Thanks. I get it."

The elevator stopped and the door hissed open. Naim exited in the underground garage which housed three vehicles. A glass wall separated the garage from a full gym and fourteen-meter pool. Naim, a health-nut, swam three days a week, weight trained two days and jogged two days. He tossed the bags into the sedan's trunk, sent a text to his driver, and rejoined Marco in the elevator. They rode up a level.

"How's your shoulder feeling?" Naim asked, making their way to the kitchen.

"A little pain. I didn't sleep well due to the severity of the discomfort. The doctor prescribed Vicodin, which made me lethargic, so I won't be taking that."

June, their motherly maid/cook, said, "Tylenol should work. We don't need you addicted to those pain pills. The epidemic is real."

"Ain't that the truth," Naim said, sitting at the table.

June slid a coffee mug in front of Naim and poured him a cup of black coffee.

June was a short, svelte woman, sporting curly white hair, and sixty-something. She didn't have children, but lived with her husband of thirty-five years in a Park Avenue apartment, minutes from Naim who was like a son. "Got little eggs scrambled with cheddar cheese, home fries, and smoked salmon."

"I'm in," Marco said, smiling. "Amber will be down shortly."

"I hope more dressed than you," June said, chuckling.

Marco said, "You're too much, Mama June." She had instructed him to call her June—No Mrs. Required. He had added "mama" out of respect. He sipped orange juice, and then asked his father, "So what case are you chasing all the way in Washington?"

"Washington?" said June perplexed. Her head was cocked to the side with a suspicious eye looking through Naim.

"Yup, I caught him taking bags to his Benz. Trying to sneak out on us."

Naim chortled. "You two are too much." He took a bite of eggs and chewed slowly.

"Stall tactic," June said, smirking. "Spill it, mister."

"If you two must know, the justice's killer called me last night and wants to meet."

"Get the eff outta here," Marco said with his jaw on the table.

"Watch the language," June demanded.

"Eighteen is not that grown for profanity, sir, and you have a vast vocabulary. Use it," Naim said.

"Back on subject," June said, tapping Naim's shoulder, "Why you? You've only been an attorney a few months."

"Two." That was the prince.

"And haven't led a case," June said with a sassy hand on her hip. Although the part-time house servant, she was more grandmother than maid.

"This no doubt will be a capital case. Can you handle that?" Marco asked bluntly.

"Yes I can," Naim replied, smiling. "It's more like a chat. Nothing says I'll take on the case per se. But to talk to this man is interesting to me."

"I got one question, counselor," Marco said skeptically. "Why'd the killer call you? Shouldn't he be trying to bring Johnny Cochran back?"

"Perhaps I am Johnny. The next JC."

"I've always loved your confidence, champ," June said, massaging his shoulders. "I want hourly updates to assure your safety."

"I want the same, dad. I gotta be honest. I don't want you involved with this monster. Police are on the hunt for this man. They may shoot you first and ask you questions later. Deem you an accomplice. I mean have you even told the police?"

Naim was at a mini bar, pulling out a bottle of Dom Perignon. He fixed himself a mimosa and retook a seat at the table.

It felt like he was engaged in an interrogation.

"No, I didn't. Attorney client privilege."

"Umm…new flash…He not a client, dad." His voice was on the side of aggression.

Naim glared at June, apparently for help.

"I'm out of this one," she said, pressing her back to the island and folding her arms over her breasts. She wanted an answer, too.

"Marco, I'm going to DC to negotiate. Negotiate for the man to turn himself in to authorities. And possibly represent him in preliminary interrogation with federal agents. I want to keep the man alive. I have to defend those who need it and this man desperately needs it. A DC lawyer will sell him out."

"He killed a Supreme Court Justice for crying-out-loud dad. Do you really want to campaign for this guy?"

"I do," Naim said, hearing the front doorbell ring. "He needs a vigorous defense like any other defendant. His level of weakness and delusion reeks of mental defect and I am duty bound to assure that he gets help and not warehoused in jail, the *defacto* mental asylum." He took a huge gulp of his breakfast libation, and then said, "And with that, I have to go. That's my driver at the door."

"You can go, but I promise this ain't over," Marco said and winked.

"That's fine," Naim said, grabbing his briefcase. "I like promises. Be sure to keep your doc appointment and stay away from in the front of news camera. Period."

———————

Despite the traffic it took Naim's driver forty minutes to reach JFK Airport. He exited the car at the US Airways gate while his driver sat his luggage on the curb. He pressed a crisp hundred dollar tip into the man's hand before entering the airport's lobby. He was met by Brandy Scott wearing huge sunglasses and a baseball cap.

He hugged her, and then said, "On the run, Beyoncé? Should I be in an airport with you?"

She laughed, and said, "Everyone is looking for me. I'm wanted for questioning—"

"By the police?"

"No," she said, smiling. "Other news agencies. My article was widely disseminated and people want to know how I obtained and confirmed that the photos of the justice were authentic."

"That's a fair question." He was smiling at the absurdity of his skeptical eye.

"You're crazy," she said jokingly, punching him. "I checked us in for the flight online. Download the US Air app for an electronic boarding pass. You can flash the pass right on your phone screen. We're in first-class, so we should get through security swiftly."

"Perfect," he said, walking towards security, "and thanks for buying the ticket."

"No problem," she said and pat his butt. "You can repay me later, handsome."

"Can you handle any more of this anaconda?" he asked, winking at her and smiling.

She grinned and he held her hand. Two love birds on a stroll through the busy airport. In her mind, no one was in the airport but them.

"We're staying at the Trump International Hotel. It's about a mile from the White House. This is a work trip, but I say we make time for pleasure. Visit King Memorial and the Smithsonian."

"That's all free, so I'm game for that," she said, and then added, "I've not sure who the hell we're meeting, but otherwise we will have a good time."

"It'll be the best." He sounded confident, but he knew who they planned to meet controlled their visit to the nation's capital.

CHAPTER 18

Not far from the White House and housed in the Old Post office lied the luxe Trump International Hotel. In a 1899 Romanesque Revival Building, the hotel offered the Grand Lobby which boasted a soaring nine-story atrium dripping with rich jewel tones—deep red, aubergine, sapphire and emerald. The area was elegantly finished with gold accent, hand-woven area rugs, soaring brass fixtures and crystal chandeliers.

Naim and Brandy checked into the palatial hotel and a doorman ushered them to a suite on the hotel's top floor, behind a pair of double doors.

"Must be big in there for French doors," Brandy whispered.

"It is," the doorman said. "Sixty-three hundred square feet."

The door was opened for them and they walked into a huge living room area. The opulent, Federal-style suite possessed high ceilings, a marble bathroom and fireplace. "Welcome to the Presidential suite," the doorman said, smiling. "For your pleasure, prominently located on the mezzanine and overlooking the iconic Clock Tower is BLT Prime. The steakhouse is phenomenal. The National Mall and the National Gallery of Art are a twelve-min walk away. Where would you like your bags?"

"In the bedroom will be fine," Naim said, and then added, "thank you, I got it from there." Naim gave the doorman a fifty.

Knowing he planned on being in town a few days, Naim decided to unpack his bags and put things into dresser drawers. His pieces from the garment bag were hung neatly in the closet. Brandy handed him her bag to hang her things, also.

"Thanks sweetie," she said, walking to the room's floor-to-ceiling window and pulling back the curtains.

Is that a test? he thought. Certainly, hanging her garments wasn't a problem. Despite their short nine months together it was already 'Til death do us part and for richer or poorer—for him anyway. No doubt, he felt that she returned the sentiment, driving him closer to her. He had an aunt who had met a man at a drug rehab center. Upon their release and recovery, he proposed to her after only three months of dating. Twenty-two years later, they remained happily married. Naim wanted that with Brandy. Two kids. And a partridge in a pear tree.

"Amazing."

"What?"

"The view," she said, looking out at the top of the White House. "Naim, come look at this view."

He walked over and found himself on the balcony with his arms wrapped around her waist. He pressed his hands against her thighs. "That's the US Treasury Building and beyond that is the White House." He pointed, and said, "And that little figure pacing up there is prepared to take out anyone daring to defy the White House's security."

"This is beautiful. How much was this suite a night?" she asked with her head twisted to face him. She kept her back tight against his chest. Each time he moved she felt his muscles contract and enjoyed the feeling. "Never mind," she said, looking at his bushy raised eyebrow. "I don't want to know. I really have to get used to a man, well not a man, *you*, being able to take care of yourself and me. And you genuinely enjoy it. I actually feel it."

"You do have to get used to it. I didn't ask how much did first-class tickets cost to get us here."

"Touché," she said, spinning around to face him.

His hands roamed until they cupped her ass. She parked her hands on his chest. He made them jump, staring into her eyes.

They shared a kiss. A deep French kiss. They could read each other's mind and their intimate intuition was a *code red* whenever they were in the other's space. It was effortless and indicative of what they'd wanted for years but had never found. They weren't looking for love and an accidentally stumbled upon their soulmates.

Pulling apart, she said, "You smell excellent. What is that you're wearing?"

"Mount Blanc Legend. And thanks," he said, looking at a crowd of picketers outside of the White House. "I wonder what they're protesting about?"

She looked at her watch, and said, "That's the first part of the Americans for Sentencing Reform protest. They're going to the SC next."

"You know, I'm all for sentencing and criminal justice reform. I continue on the Families Against Mandatory Minimums board. But I don't get why people have the right to protest on the grounds of the White House. That space should be respected a tad more."

"This isn't China or North Korea?"

"With this scenario it should be. Besides, the president is probably inside numb, caring less and less about this issue continuing to plague our community. You see FAMM pressed issues on the Congressional floor and submitted an amicus brief to the Supreme Court. Black people protest loudly and are often not heard."

"You may be right, but I'm sure the president is briefed daily on who has a permit to be outside voicing their political positions."

"Right," he said not looking to debate. They've had their share of political disagreements and now was not a time to exert energy on friendly arguing. "How 'bout room service? Out here on the balcony," he asked, pivoting to the next topic like a seasoned politician. "We can eat and admire the view."

"Ignoring those hugs box things strategically placed on the White House roof," she said, smiling.

"Yup, don't do anything outrageous, because the boxes contain surface-to-air missiles that will blow this room and that pretty little face of yours to smithereens."

———————

After sautéed boneless chicken breast, buttered squash, and sweet potato fries, Naim was on the bed relaxing. His eyes switched between watching Brandy at the room's desk working on her laptop, and watching the continual loop of CNN's BREAKING NEWS, which wasn't breaking any longer. The redundant use of the "Breaking News" banner undermined the true meaning of the phrase. For Naim, it was like crying wolf. Bottom line, the Columbia U shooting and the justice's murder were a day old and no longer breaking.

"I get so lonely," Naim said, singing the infamous Janet Jackson tune.

Brandy's head whipped in his direction. She smiled.

"You're too damn much." She blew him a kiss. "Almost done over here, but you know, I have to be on the SC portico soon."

"You?" He sat up. "We. I'm gong."

"You're not. If he sees you, he may not talk to me," she said, walking over to the bed. She pushed him back and straddled on top of him. Looking into his eyes, she said, "Listen, I'm going to be fine. This is normal for me to meet bad guys." She kissed him. "You're my number one bad guys."

"I don't shoot people," he replied, smiling. He still hadn't told her that he was slated to represent the same bad guy in a court of law.

CHAPTER 19

Washington, D.C.—Medical Examiner's Office

Detective McGee pulled into a parking space outside of the Department of Forensic Sciences. The building housed several divisions of the Metropolitan PD, including the Firearms and Fingerprint Examination Division, DNA Laboratory, and the Forensic Sciences Services division. They were there for an eleven o'clock appointment with Deputy Medical Examiner, Dr. Henry Butterfield. The building in front of them was a modern D.C. architecture. Wide and high, cream marble, stone, slate, black metal window frames, and black handrails along a handicap ramp leading to the entrance.

"I love this place," Detective McGee said to her partner, hopping out of the car. She threw on her sunglasses.

"Always gloom and doom despite the sun shining brightly," Detective Bald Eagle said, shielding her eyes from the sun. "What do you think we'll learn? Anything to get us closer to the suspect?"

"I hope so. Any additional details will help. I really want to know why those two men were naked in the bedroom with a wife steps away," Detective McGee replied, approaching the reception desk.

They announced their business and was told to wait for Dr. Butterfield's assistant to scoop them from the lobby.

———————

Dr. Henry Butterfield had reported to his office to autopsy Chief Weston at five a.m. He had been to the crime scene, recorded the position of the bodies found, and took a preliminary survey of the deceased. He was pleased with the forensics unit and responding MPD officer's ability to record and preserve the scene and bodies. Upon settling at his desk, he e-mailed the head of the forensics division and the captain of the police district, congratulating them on doing a fine job too assure they'd nab the killer.

Afterward he got into clean scrubs, surgical mask, washed his hands, gloved-up, and started reviewing the judge's body and the male found at the scene in the Weston's bedroom. The man dressed in the judge's gown was fortunate to have to died swiftly. He was in possession of a gavel, and looking at the justice's buttocks Dr. Butterfield learned where the gavel had been put to use, possibly before the arrival of the killer. He had withdrawn one unit of whole blood from both victims and was waiting on in-house toxicology results to be returned.

He had begun preparing recorded notes of his autopsy findings some hours later when the lab's phone rang. A technician informed him that the detectives were there to meet with him. He had met them on

Twenty-eight street, N.W. in Georgetown, and was struck by how handsome the women were. They were ingrained in his memory.

When the tech ushered the detectives into his office, Dr. Butterfield was behind his desk flipping through papers in a folder he had prepared for the detectives; a parting gift. Dr. Butterfield was in his sixties, pure white and gray hair, albino complexion, tall, emaciated, with coffee-tinted teeth.

The sounds of their voices and the scent of their presence mesmerized him. He stood and shook both women's hands. Soft. Delicate. Warm.

"Delighted. Please sit down," the doctor said, smiling.

"Thank you," Detective McGee said, having a seat. She sat a recorder in her lap and pressed record. "Just to memorialize our conversation. This not a deposition and will not be used in any legal proceeding."

"Will not or cannot?" he asked. "In Washington, there is a difference."

"Cannot," she replied, shrugging with a sarcastic grin on her face.

"Just checking. The autopsy isn't complete by any stretch, but I've made findings that may aid your pursuit of the killer. Surely, I want to get the perpetrator captured forthwith."

Both women nodded. They were there for the meat and potatoes and didn't need the doctor's wish list.

"Can we see the body?" Detective Bald Eagle said, removing her sunglasses to look the doctor in the eyes. She adored death.

"Sure, but let's discuss some things that are odd," he said, scanning the contents of the folder that he had prepared for them. He pushed it across his desk towards to McGee. She appeared to be the lead detective. He didn't know for sure, but the recorder's presence gave it away. "Opening to the first page. You'll see the results of instant toxicology and serology tests. Of course, the full screen will be back in about a month. We found no cocaine or alcohol in Weston's body, but he had ingested cannabinoids prior to his death."

"No coke, but smoking weed?" McGee asked, frowning.

"Well, sources of cannabinoids are marijuana or hemp, but that's not my concern. It wasn't smoked. It's a usual material to ingest."

"Hmmm."

"As you know a nude man was found in the judge's bedroom," the doctor said, raising his eyebrows. "Perhaps our judge who opposed the legalization of gay marriage was gay himself."

"Smokescreen, huh? Masking his own sexuality. Fraud." Detective Bald Eagle was shaking her head.

"Don't be so mean," Detective McGee said. "Continue doctor."

"Both men tested positive for H.I.V., but that status does not, in any way, change my option that blunt force trauma to the head was what killed the judge."

The detectives looked at each other.

Detective McGee asked, "I know the autopsy isn't complete, but are you asserting with a reasonable degree of medical certainty that he died from the injuries we've seen on the scene?"

"Yes," the doctor said. "Let's go look at the body. There are a few interesting things," he added, rubbing his hands together. Pure excitement on his face. *Ah, the joy of dead bodies.*

A moment later, they stood in front of a *death refrigerator* and the doctor pulled out the slab where the judge rested with a y-shaped incision in his chest. A tag dangled from his big toe, his morgue driver's license card. Gone was all of his fancy credentials and his color—his caramel complexion had blanched. His chest was cut open starting at the shoulders, meeting in between his sagging chest, and then sliced to his pelvis forming the Y. A severely bruised face surrounded dead eyes that stared up at them. And the judge's penis was gone.

"Should his eyes still be open?" Detective Bald Eagle asked.

"Nope," the doctor said, slipping on gloves and shutting them. "There we go. Photographic slides of his pupils were taken to depict the judge's statement for a potential jury."

"His last photo shoot."

"Precisely," the doctor said. "Judge Percy Weston endured multiplied blunt force injuries to the head, neck, torso, and upper extremities. Four laceration or tears to the top and left eye, multiple fractures to the skull that penetrated his brain. A fracture of the spine, and a fracture of the hyoid bone." He took a breath.

"And what might that be? Hyoid bone?"

"The horseshoe-shaped bone that sits in the upper part of the neck. It's an injury consistent with a strangulation. However, the cause of death was not strangulation in this case."

"But he was strangled?"

"Yes, and nearly decapitated undoubtedly inflicted by the du-rag wrapped tightly around his neck."

"Du-rag?" Astonished.

The doctor nodded, facing Detective McGee. "The other injuries are consistent with what would have been caused by the hammer found at the scene. It's unlikely that any other possible weapons recovered at the scene caused these blunt force injuries."

"Must have been a lot of force?"

"Significant force indeed, but not for these," the doctor said, signaling for an assistant to join them. Dr. Butterfield's assistant pressed eight-by-ten photographs into his huge hands. They were pictures of the judge's ass. "Someone was being spanked with a gavel. Presumably, by Dorian Jackson since he was found with the gavel in hand."

The detectives looked at the judge's rear end which was riddled with two-inch round circles with the initials "PW" in the center of them.

"I'm thinking the perp walked in on a sexual fantasy being fulfilled," Detective McGee said. "That's why Dorian was in the robe. Perhaps that part wasn't staged?"

"Hence, the seeming crime of passion that has taken place. I mean the killer had a gun, but killed them with a hammer," Bald Eagle said.

"I'd say your guy is huge," the doctor added.

Detective Bald Eagle reasoned that, "The judge was gay, the wife knew it, allowed it. Maybe they were just married because in the US certainly a Supreme Court judge cannot get divorced. That would require a reason and normally an immoral reason and God knows an immoral person cannot sit on the highest court. Perhaps this wasn't a political kill. Or they were having a threesome. Or this all stagecraft."

"To be or not to be," the doctor said, smiling. He covered the corpse with a white sheet, and said, "All of this is off the record until I send you and the AUSA—who's been begging for me to get this done—a copy of my completed findings."

"AUSA?"

"Yes, the case has been assigned to Shai Brown. You didn't know?"

"Yes," Detective Bald Eagle said, lying.

CHAPTER 20

After a rowdy mid-day romp, Brandy dressed, and Naim admired her curves that seeped through her jeans and T-shirt. She was an in-shape woman that had planned ahead for a rally by the looks of her sneakers and New York Yankees fitted cap, covering her hair pulled into a ponytail.

He kissed her goodbye at the suite's door. "Be safe," he suggested, "and hurry back. I didn't come to D.C. to be alone."

"Neither did I," she said. "I'll be back by dinner time."

"OK, I'll book a table somewhere nice. We can have a drink here first and then head out."

"Perfect," she said, and she was gone.

When she reached the valet stand and spoke to an attendant, he pointed to an SUV at the hotel's curb with a driver standing next to it. The French man held a sheet of paper with *B. Scott* on it. Making eye contact with the driver, he nodded opened the back door for her, but she walked around the car once and recorded the license plate number in her iPhone Notes app. A habit she did with all taxi, Uber, or other drivers that were strangers. She felt that she was in capable hands because Naim had hired a security firm that Baker and Keefe represented to whisk her around the city. The same security firm that sold Naim his armored Cadillac Escalade to protect him. This after he was shot at during an incident, escaping bullets from some woman that he had engaged in sex with while her husband was at work.

The veteran newswoman hopped into the back seat, and said, "This makes my trip to the court seem like a dangerous mission."

"Well, ma'am," the driver said, locking the doors, "Americans for Sentencing Reform, despite their mission and motive are notorious for forcing riot gear and gas masks to come out. I assure you, you'll be safe from both, and bullets, in this tank." He pulled off of the hotel curb, and asked, "Air conditioning?"

Naim, dressed in all black, despite the heat, shot out of the hotel's entrance like a bullet out of a pistol. He stopped under the US flags flying over the entrance. Looking around he found a young couple approaching a taxi, passed them a fifty and said, "I really need this cab," while hopping into the back seat. To the driver, he said, "Follow that SUV," slamming the door shut. "And don't worry about being seen. The driver knows I'm behind him."

CHAPTER 21

Americans for Sentencing Reform was founded in 2010 to take aggressive action on sentencing reform. It was a strategic threat to all politicians. It had a simple threat for politicians: Draft legislation to help low-class citizens or be voted out of office the next term, no matter party affiliation. They wanted elected officials to make good on all of their promises made on the campaign trail. ASR leaders proposed legislation to officials and if they were Democrat and didn't get it onto the Congressional floor they instructed all members to vote for the opposing party the next election. They were setting congressional term limits since politicians didn't do it on their own.

Federal law made it unlawful to parade, stand, or move in processions or assemblages in the Supreme Court Building or grounds; ASR protestors were on the Court's elevated marble plaza violating said law. The plaza's features convey in many distinctive ways that a person had entered some special type of enclave. It served what amounted to the elevated front porch of the Supreme Court, complete with a surrounding railing. The tranquil environment was being molested by ASR members that held signs and banners designed to bring into public notice their organization and movement; also in violation of *40 United States Crimes Code 6135*. The statute encompassed not only the building, but also the four streets surrounding it, the plaza, and the surrounding promenade, lawn area and steps. Despite this, ASR members weren't deterred. No doubt, Supreme Court Police were aggravated and prepared to disperse the thick crowds of people comprising of a multitude of minority races.

David Thurman was amongst them, undoubtedly standing out from the crowd. An hour earlier he had been asked to leave for passing out ASR leaflets on court's property. He was back and in costume. The local Fox News affiliated justice correspondent stopped him, stuck a microphone in his face, and asked, "Excused me, sir, what are you wearing?" She's sounded like a fashionista stalking celebrity on the Academy Award's red carpet.

"Oh, this is Gianni Versace," Thurman said, forcing himself and the correspondent to laugh at the ludicrous lie. "No seriously, this costume is constructed using various materials from the District of Columbia environment, including newspapers, shampoo bottles, and empty honey jars. It's all been wrapped in duct tape, forming into this bullet-proof vest shape of my chest." He spins three hundred sixty degrees, and said, "I hope you like." He did a masculine curtsy, then, held up a small, hand-carved mask sculpture, and said. "For entertainment purposes."

"Don't you think the police will be concerned with you wearing a mask in the wake of a justice of the Court being murdered and the constant threat of a terrorist attack. I mean," the reporter said, grimacing, "There is an atmosphere of heightened anxiety and concerns over safety and security in the capital."

Thurman stepped back and put the mask to his face, securing it with strings that wrapped around his ears. "Look," he said, his voice coming through a slit in the mask, muffling his voice. "This is America and we need to be tolerant of our people. That embraces the Constitution. Not live in this hate-filled, partisan society crammed with overzealousness and suspicion. This mask and costume are being worn to study people's interactions with me and to spread the lost concept of tolerance and understanding while we fight for reform that affects all Americans, both black and white people."

"But you're on the ground of the highest court with this chicanery."

"Yes, a court that has an important hearing coming up on making a sentencing reform retroactive to right some of the wrongs done by a liberal Congress during the forty years that they led the House of Representatives. As you know Judge Weston, is dead, God bless him, leaving an eight-judge panel split into two. Four conservatives. Four liberals. The playing field had been balanced."

"By a ruthless coward killer," the reporter said, batting her eyes.

"Name calling won't get you very far. The killer is listening to you," Thurman said, smiling wickedly.

"And, you may be right. But with Chief Weston gone, conservatives need a liberal judge to side with them to settle the lower court's split amongst the circuits."

"Now you might be right, but I strongly believe that justice for all will be accomplished. As a white American, I can confidently say when harsh sentencing laws affect the children of white soccer moms in rural Maine, the wheels of justice tend to quicken."

"We've got to leave it there," the reporter said, "but I appreciate your time."

"It was a pleasure," Thurman said, walking away.

He sent a text to Brandy Scott indicating for her to meet him in the Crypt area of the Capitol Building. She replied that she'd see him there. Grinning, he texts back: I'm headed there to shake things up.

———

Two Capitol policeman whispered and snickered, watching foolishly dressed David Thurman enter the Capitol Building doors. Standing in the security line, he rocked on his heels with his hands behind his back, cavalierly whistling an old show tune: Three Company. Scrutinizing his costume Officer Allie suspiciously asked about his costume's purpose.

"Doing research."

"For?"

"Look, I'm an artist doing research for an upcoming performance."

"Don't get snappy," replied the cop, signaling for Thurman to step up to pass through several security checkpoints.

Admission into the highly secure Capitol Building was quite a task. The lives of five hundred thirty-eight Congress members demanded an entrance equipped with a magnetometer, x-ray machine, and explosive detectors. All had to be cleared by Thurman, *The Performer*. And he did with all eyes on him from policeman and other visitors.

Just above the newer chambers in the building stood galleries where visitors watched the Senate and House of Representatives. Thurman was inside of one and had captured the attention of visitors as he performed for them. He danced and sang as visitors took photos and videos of him. Some even posed in pictures with him. Autographs were given out on pamphlets he had clandestinely smuggled into the building. The material he gave to visitors informed them about federal sentencing reform and asked them to contact their representatives to request that they pass House Bill S.5682, FIRST STEP Act.

"Thank you," Brandy said after he handed her a leaflet. "I see you're performing." It was not hard for her to surmise that the actor was her guy.

"Well, it's a rehearsal for my stage play 'David/Dafidi.' The best way to do it based on my philosophy that Life is a Performance."

She held her hand out for him to shake. He did, and she asked, "You must be my guy?" It was really just to confirm.

"I am," he said, bowing as if it was a curtain call. "Glad you could make it."

"I am a New Yorker and never miss a performance. Tell me," she said, smiling. "What's all this really about?" She wanted to get to the core of their tête-à-tête before it was broken up.

"My wife," he said, nodding his head to a corner of the Crypt area where no one else was. "She's in federal jail for what many would call a petty drug offense, but was given a mandatory fifteen-year and eight-months because she was deemed a career offender."

"I know a little about this," she said, looking him in his eyes. She wanted him to understand that she was listening.

"I'm aware that you do. Our linking is not by accident. I read your article on the topic and your coverage of the Families Against Mandatory Minimums concert put on in New York last summer. My wife Jillian loved it, also."

"Thank you both. I'm dating someone on the FAMM board, so I have an inside track to much of the goings on with them."

"ASR, which I am the secret leader of, is a tad different, Ms. Scott. We're more aggressive than FAMM. I'm not truly a monster, but I'm prepared to die and pay back all parties responsible for my wife rotting away at FCI Alderson. I know you'll have to turn me in, but before you do, I'm begging you to help me expose these cowards that are destroying the lives of many Americans. I know we like to make this a black versus white disparity issue. And some like to say white people only get involved when it hits home for us. Differences aside we have a problem of us versus them—police and lawmakers—and until the public at large understand this problem, it won't stop for white families like mine or black families like yours."

"Excuse me," Officer Preston Crowder of the Capitol Police asked, approaching them. His uniform exposed bulging biceps and he sported a menacing bald head. "Two Things. What are you holding? And you're not allowed to pass out material on the Capitol grounds or the SC grounds which you've been warned of earlier.

"This object," Thurman said, holding up the mask, is a hand-carved mask sculpture."

"Drop the mask," Officer Crowder said. "Then, you must leave and cease giving out any more leaflets, which you've now been told a second time."

Brandy backed away from the ensuing confrontation.

"I'm not giving you anything, and—"

Officer Crowder violently jerked the mask from Thurman's hand and slammed it to the floor. It shattered startling Capitol visitors who looked shocked as the killer delivered a barbaric blow to the cop's solar plexus. When the cop folded over, Thurman grabbed his head and drove it into the wall.

Brandy's cellphone was out recording the madness—an investigator at work.

Before other officers arrived, a bystander kicked Thurman in the back forcing his body to slam into Officer Crowder. They both hit the floor, and the spectator kicked Thurman in his head and limbs, freeing the officer from his confused state and allowing him to whip out his gun. He fired two shots.

CHAPTER 22

It took the detectives a half hour to bounce through the capital in the Impala. The car windows were down, catching warm wind as they zipped to the United States Attorney's office in Judiciary Square. Detective McGee parked in a private garage, before walking two blocks to the prosecutor's office. They rode an elevator to the sixth floor, approached a receptionist behind a bulletproof glass, and announced their business. They were asked to wait in a bland, carpeted lobby with eighties wood paneling and framed headshots of the sitting US President and current US Attorney General on the wall.

Waiting to meet the Big Kahuna, they whispered toxic, demeaning rhetoric about the man they were set to meet. Leonardo Gucci had been with the office since God had passed along the Ten Commandments;

yet, he was passed over for the head job and took it out on police officers and uncooperative defendants. He appeared at the security door, wearing his familiar frown. A blustery Italian man with an outrageous comb-over of blonde hair and a ruddy complexion. He spent more time in the tanning salon, then, the gym. Obviously. But he possessed, despite being the second-in-charge, a name that appeared as the prosecution for almost every noteworthy murder in the District over the past twenty years. His grand list of criminals behind bars was impressive.

After passing through metal detectors—reserved for confidential informants and outsiders—-they huddled in Leonardo Gucci's office. Sitting at a six-person conference table was AUSA Shai Brown.

"Ladies…" Brown began, smiling. "Have a seat," he said, pointing to seats at the conference table. Brown had a dark complexion, dark hazel eyes, and perfect teeth.

"Make it Detective McGee and Bald Eagle," Detective McGee said deadpan.

"OK, if that's how you want to play it." He had a super sardonic aura to complement an upper-class education with a year abroad at Oxford University.

"I do," she replied. There was constant tension between her and Brown, a man she'd once casually dated. "Can we get to the business of capturing Justice Weston's Killer?" She crossed her legs in a cheap leather chair.

"We hear you have a substantial lead for us to follow up on?" Detective Bald said, running her middle finger across her eyebrow.

"We do, but we must preface this discussion by confirming, I mean, they're papers filed, a suit, claiming you, Detective McGee, caused intentional infliction of emotional stress and maliciously prosecuted a woman," AUSA Brown said with a supreme sneer on his face.

While seated at his desk, AUSA Gucci added, "You can imagine how that'll complicate this matter if you're called testify at trial."

Detective McGee was silent, staring blankly out a tinted window into a sunny D.C. sky. She set her sight on the apex of the Washington Monument. Let freedom ring.

AUSA Brown railed on, flipping through a sheaf of papers in a folder. He said, "In 2002 you obtained—"

"A false confession from a Carol Jackson using coercive interrogation tactics. You also…allegedly…suppressed and disregarded evidence demonstrating her innocence of the murder she was charged with committing. This office withdrew prosecution, and then, arrested and convicted the true murderers—"

"That's what we do," AUSA Gucci chimed in, looking up from his computer.

"Despite this…um…allegation," AUSA Brown said, "you became a lecturer and teacher on police interrogation tactics last year, and have been recorded admitting that you had coerced her confession and had disregarded evidence that was exculpatory. It's on video, ma'am." Brown closed the folder and set it aside. He tented his hands on the table, leering at Detective McGee.

"The Metropolitan Police Department expressed that you were assigned to lead this case by rotation. And your commander is confident that you're explicitly capable of handling the vigor of a case on this scale." He had a seat at the head of the table, and added, "I just need assurances from you that you'll play this by the book because there's a lot riding on this case. We cannot give people the impression that they can kill our people sans consequence. Severe consequences."

After briefly digesting his word, Detective Bald Eagles said, "I'm sure your elevation to D.C. U.S. Attorney is riding on this. It's widely known you're set to replace the top man of this office who is awaiting Senate confirmation to join the D.C. District Court as the first Mexican-American on the bench here in the city. This case is a must win for you to go to your bosses post."

"You can deduce," ASUA Gucci said, adjusting in his seat. "We must, though, acknowledge that I can win this without you two."

Brown said, "The FBI Assistant Special Agent in Charge is a stone throw away and can assume responsibility of this case because of the victim. Under that scenario you go back to you MPD district and I go on to head this office. Win-win for me." He smiled and adjusted his power-tie.

"Not so fast," Detective McGee said. Everyone had spoked and it was her turn. "You've forgotten one small detail. Your office has to defend the claim levied against me. If we lose, the floodgates would open and many of the other black and brown defendants in Southeast DC will be rich for mistakes like the one I've made. So how about we cut the bullshit and get to the business at hand as I've stated moments ago."

The two men in the room looked at each other. The two women did the same. Lines were drawn and smirks settled on everyone's faces.

"We can get to business," AUSA Gucci said, "but know that this case must be played by the very playbook you teach from Detective, McGee."

"Got it," she said, cocking her head to the side.

Reaching under the table, AUSA Gucci retrieved an attaché. He opened and pulled out a CD. He rolled in his chair to a TV with a DVD player, popped in the cd, and pressed PLAY. On the screen a man appeared at an ATM machine, inserting a card into it and withdrawing cash.

"That's our man," AUSA Brown said, at the screen, "using the judges' debit card. He's on the loose with a four hundred dollar head start."

CHAPTER 23

The shots forced David Thurman to freeze. He was on the floor, back against the wall at gunpoint, two bullets holes in the floor on both sides of his body.

Ethnicity saved his life. His lucky day.

Thirty to forty officers converged in the Crypt area, including members of the Capitol Police Hazardous Device Unit, the Federal Bureau of Investigation Joint Terrorism Task Force, and Detective William Bosswick who had handcuffed Thurman. Detective Bosswick wore a boring buzz cut and was known to have steroid induced spurts of violence. Thurman's costume was cautiously being cut from his body, as Detective Bosswick asked, "Are there any wires or explosives in your costume?"

"No," Thurman said through clenched teeth. He was face down on the ground with an officer's knee in his back and another on his neck, as he was aggressively frisked.

"I'm wearing it for artistic purposes. Is that a crime?"

"I'll let you know," Detective Bosswick said, "but know that the only performers in this building have senator or representative in front of their name."

Watching an officer leave the area, gingerly carrying the costume, Thuman asked, "Where are you taking my property?"

"To be x-rayed and preliminary testing to determine if it contains any explosives, chemical agents, or radiation."

Thurman snickered. "Wasn't that tested prior to my admission?"

"In the interim you're going to be taken to the Capitol Hill Police Processing Center, interrogated, and arrested."

"That's fine," Thurman said, grinning into Brandy's camera. "Lawyer please."

David Thurman was strip-searched and police confiscated a set of car keys, which had been matched to a 2003 Ford Expedition. Police located the van in the three hundred block of Third Street NE, four blocks from the Capitol Building. Because his costume resembled a vest associated with a suicide bomber, there was concern that there may be explosives inside of the truck. Perhaps, there were explosives inside of the truck, because the suspect may have been engaging in a "dry run" to test security, observe response procedures, and capabilities at the Capitol Building.

Capitol Police, Kevin Malloy, looked at the truck, and recorded the out-of-state license plate, before looking inside of it. It was filthy, and he said to his captain, "I think he lives out of this thing. The plate is from New York. I'll assume he's from there."

Daniel Finnerty, the Commander of the Hazardous Incident Response Division of the Capitol Police, simply furrowed his brows. An intelligent reply. The captain wore a crisp suit over his taut, tawny physique. After canvassing the neighborhood he was informed that neighbors and restaurant employees had agreed that the truck had been parked in the same location since at least nine a.m.

A canine search of the van's exterior didn't reveal any traces of explosives, but while conducting the search canine officers observed large containers in the rear of the van covered by blankets and clothing. Captain Finnerty ordered that the entire block where the van was parked be cleared of vehicular and pedestrian traffic. Neighbors were told to go the backside of their homes and seek cover until someone knocked on their doors. He then OK'd bomb technicians to perform a diagnostic inspection of the van's exterior and interior to determine if the vehicle contained explosives or other hazardous materials. He was determined to nail, David Thurman, to the top the Capitol Building.

Donning protective equipment to safeguard themselves from exposure to any hazard chemicals, agents entered the van. Inspecting the vans interior, they confirmed that the large containers presented in the back of the van were filled with urine. None of the containers had attached wired and were packed in HAZMAT-approved containers, leaving them inside of the van.

Clearing the blocks of its lockdown status, Captain Finnerty consulted with Alexander Morgan a supervisor at the FBI's Washington Field Office, who ordered him to have the truck impounded and towed to an FBI storage facility.

After the call, he was informed that David Thurman's lawyer had arrived.

"Sucks to be him or her," the captain said, tilting his head to the side.

CHAPTER 24

Detective Bald Eagle sat in silence because she nor her partner had anything as significant as the AUSA to report. Usually she brought the assistant United States Attorney evidence or facts to have a warrant drafted to execute on a bank demanding that they turned over surveillance. But they'd beat her to the punch and that was surprising. The US Attorney's office had miles of corridors and thousands of square feet of office space, all occupied by legal carnivores, but the bombshells needed to sharpen their teeth was typically garnered by detectives like her, so their revelation was vexing, and a blow to her ego.

"Care to tell us how you've so swiftly come across this video?" Detective McGee asked.

"That's a good place to start," AUSA Brown said. He slid a Manila envelope across the table. "Was sent over by courier late morning. A gift."

"Not really. We don't know who sent it," Detective Bald Eagle said.

"That's your job to find out," AUSA Brown said. "The courier service is located at Wisconsin Avenue and M. Street in Georgetown. The manager is waiting on you to grab up surveillance of the sender."

"I'm going to take a wild-ass guess and assume you've contacted the bank to verify authenticity?" Detective McGee asked.

"We have. Two things. Yes, it's genuine, but it's known to be off ten-to fifteen-minutes. I've talked to the branch manager," AUSA Brown said. "A gentlemen passing as an FBI Agent secured it. They have a video of him, too. He's in a ball cap, aviator glasses and a thick beard. Obviously, all three are designed to thwart facial recognition technology. The beard may be fake or even shaved off by now according to the manager. There was also a question as to whether he was a white man with a tan or a high-yellow black man."

"Fair question, considering the bank's location. It's a Bank of America in Southeast," Detective McGee said.

"This guy could really be trying to throw us into the wrong direction," Detective Bald Eagle said. "Why not a bank in a white neighborhood over in Virginia. Why choose a very black section of the city to pilfer the judge's account?"

"Maybe the ATM user is not the actual killer, but an accomplice?" Detective McGee replied.

AUSA Gucci listened. All quiet. This was not a brainstorming session. Cutting everyone off, he said, "I've prepared a press release, titled, *Suspect(s) sought in Judge Weston's Homicide*. I've included the following statement: "Minutes after the murder an unidentifiable white male used Judge Weston's bank card at an ATM at the Bank of America located in the 2100 block of Martin Luther King Avenue SE. A photograph of the subject was taken by the bank camera."

Brown said, "We're going to release the picture of this guy with the statement. We're going to send it all media outlets, but it should be featured on the cover of the *Washington Post* and *Washington Times* bright and early tomorrow morning."

"And to your point," AUSA Gucci said, "if he is trying, and, I do mean trying, to throw us off by using an ATM is Southeast, but staying in a posh Washington hotel, he'll know that we mean business when his photo is slipped under every hotel room door in town and exposed on every newsstand. He won't be able to walk anywhere without being noticed."

Detective McGee watched the prosecutor's mannerisms. They were seriously talking about the capture of a Supreme Court justice's murder. The search would be a huge undertaking. Lots of moving parts. Therefore all plans had to be on point. They had two days max, she figured, to get their ducks in a row. Or there may not ever be a resolution.

CHAPTER 25

Brandy had the driver let her out at Constitution Avenue and Twelfth Street. She decided to walk the balance of the distance back to the hotel. Walking allowed her to think before she had acted on what she knew and observed. To write a report on what she witnessed, or not? For her, everything was news, but it was becoming a task to report subjects that called into questions the greatness of the United States. She was beginning to struggle with the idea that the public—and the United States' enemies—needed to know every morsel about national security. She hated that political scandals highlighted the flaws of the U.S. to foreigners. She passed the National Museum of American History which she ignored because she wasn't in tourism mode at that moment. She had to investigate in an effort to connect what she saw and what

David Thurman told her to facts. *Who was his wife? What were the circumstances surrounding her arrest and conviction? Who was David Thurman, really?* The costume and the acting had been perplexing. David Thurman's arrest and assault was a consequence that she had rarely ever eye-witnessed. She stopped in a discount store and bought massage bubble bath and scented candles.

She carried her purchases back to the hotel, cutting through The Ellipse, and let herself into the suite. It had been replenished. New towels—clean and plush—new wrapped moistening soap, and fresh roses had been changed. The roses were red, but the new set was yellow. She ran bath water, stripped down, and wiggled her luscious body into a four-person Jacuzzi. On the side of the tub was a silver tray with two glasses and a bottle of white Santa Margherita pinot grigio. *Lovely*, she thought. *Wait, where's Nai?*

CHAPTER 26

Naim Butler had chatted in a whisper to David Thurman in a small interview room. He feared that the room was bugged by federal authorities. It was a growing suspicion from ordinary citizens that its government went through great lengths to spy on them. Naim didn't imagine that attorney-client interview rooms were off limits. America hadn't been safer since whistleblower, Edward Snowden, skipped town for Russia. Naim wasn't taking any chances with a case already classified high profile. Their conversation was broken up by a polite little tap, tap, tappity, tap on the room's door. Naim expected a ferocious boom, boom, boom, by the big head federal agents trained to make a frightening first impression.

Naim stood up and walk to the door. He knocked on it as nicely as the person on the other side. Thurman smiled. He liked theater. No one expected a door to talk back. Definitely not at that United States Capitol.

He opened up and saw two guys in Capitol police uniforms. Both possessed side arms and looked pretty darn pissed off. Behind them was a man in a suit. David hadn't seen the man the size of a heavy-weight boxer. The man was stuffed in his suit, golden-haired, and chiseled with an aquiline nose. Perhaps he was an OK guy—it was doubtful. He nodded at the uniforms, who positioned themselves on both sides of Thurman, lifting him to his feet, and handcuffed him.

Thurman asked, "Where are you taking me?"

"Shut the hell up," the unknown man said. He turned to the suspect's counselor, and said, "Come with me, Mr. Butler."

"Don't talk to me that way," Thurman said. "Am I under arrest?"

"Must be what you want," the man said. "If so, keep on running your trap."

"Running my…look here, Goldie, make your mind up. Am I free to go with my attorney or not?"

"You asked for this." He turned to one of his officers, and said, "Take him to the interview room and read him his Miranda warnings. Skip the part about being able to afford an attorney. I'm sure Mr. Naim Butler is running him three-hundred per."

The officers walked away from the man and Naim.

Naim said, "What's your name?"

"Rudolph."

"You got a first name or title to go with that, Rudolph?"

"Why do you ask?"

"Not polite to answer a question with a question."

"I know that, so?"

"OK, first name?"

"Hank," the guy said.

"Perfect," Naim said. "Hank Rudolph."

"Is that a threat?"

"Is that what you think? My skin color lead you to that?"

"What I think certainly matters and that should scare you."

"Now that sounds like a threat."

"I'm assistant United States Attorney, Hank Rudolph, and I can make threats. Trust, I make good ones every one."

"I'll make a note of it."

"With that out of the way," the prosecutor said, "let me be clear. I'm not for any shenanigans of New York City theater."

"Then, play nice and the fireworks will stay in my briefcase."

"Fireworks are unlawful in D.C., but with your record of breaking laws, I doubt you care."

"You've found some facts and not circumstantial evidence. That's dangerous."

"Here's where we are. Your client will be charged and arraigned for unlawful entry, a violation of D.C. Code subsection 22-3302 (b), as well as the federal statute banning the display within the Capitol building of items designed to bring notice to organizations or movements."

"He hasn't unlawful entered any building."

"You seriously have some catching up to do, if you think so." The prosecutor rocked on his heels and grinned. "Now your client has some other explaining to do, but as for you, I want you to be careful here in D.C."

"Careful? Meaning?"

AUSA Rudolph spun around, began walking away, and over his shoulder said, "You're missing a helluva game, counselor. Have the cop let you out we'll see you in interview room four. Welcome to the Nation's Capital."

CHAPTER 27

Alderson, West Virginia—Federal Prison Camp Alderson

During the roaring twenties, there was a shortage of federal prison space for female inmates. Women were either slapped on the wrists or housed alone within all-male prisons; however, many of these woman were sexually abused by prison staff and fellow inmates. Alderson was opened in 1927 as the first federal women's prison in the United States. The West Virginia area was chosen for this reform movement prison because it was remote enough from major population centers, making escapes less likely.

Every morning, Jillian Thurman, completed a five-mile jog around the Alderson yard at six a.m. followed by breakfast—bran flakes that unapologetically tasted like cardboard, skim milk, and pear cut in half because God forbid an inmate made hooch with the fruit in the prison's dining hall. Truly a breakfast fueling her to make it through another day, being a stone's throw away from *Dante's Inferno*. She was beginning to look fit, having gotten rid of her stodgy pudginess with which she began her prison term seven years ago. She was in her mid-thirties, tall, five-ten, a natty, sinuous woman, with her black hair in a shoulder-length bob with bangs. Cool and reserved to the point of being frigid with just enough warmth to avoid being referred to as a total bitch, despite how appropriate. Prison had blessed her with a controlled life, calculating in every aspect, forcing her to deal with the petty officers and pointless Bureau of Prisons rules and regulations.

After breakfast and a shower, she reported to her work detail as a GED tutor. She was assigned to tutoring women in their pursuit of passing the GED test. However, many of them slept in class or read gossip magazines, because they didn't have a teacher, just her as a tutor. But weren't tutors supposed to reinforce a teacher's lessons? There was a BOP staffer assigned as the teacher, but he never taught. He was paid handsomely out of the national budget to sit in his office playing games on his computer looking up fantasy sports stats, or filling out irrelevant paperwork to indicate he was doing his job. That was the wasteful habits of many BOP position. Many of which could be eliminated and not disrupt the running of any prison. The teacher was a waste of taxpayers dollar—along with the rest of the education department. He was more babysitter than teachers, and Jillian Thurman wanted to expose him to the public.

What troubled her most was that students were required to attend class—but not do any work—or they risked losing good time release days. She surmised that they had to keep students in class, because no students, meant no need for money from taxpayers. It explained why an inmate could lose telephone, e-mail, and visiting privileges for not making a bed or having a shirt-tail tucked in; but, faced no punishment for sleeping in class. The contrast highlighted that it wasn't a *correctional* facility at all. What'd she expected from staff more appropriately suited to work the front-end of Walmart Superstore? And, sadly ordinary citizens had no clue.

Usually after work, Julian Thurman played cards, mostly poker—with wild cards—with other women in the unit's day room. They played for postage stamps, the convict's currency. Some women tried to team up against her, but mostly, she won and took their money, because growing up in Atlantic, New Jersey, she was a card counter. Also very smart. So smart she had been the maestro of the loud music being made in Washington, D.C. to have her brought before her sentencing judge and re-sentenced. Not just her, but all men and woman given draconian mandatory sentences for trafficking drugs. Each day was Groundhogs Day for her, and she didn't quite understand why a Supreme Court judge had to die for people to realize that the national federal average sentence for murder was twenty-three years, and it wasn't logical for a non-violent drug offender to be handed a LIFE-sentence, forced to languish under the faux *correctional* system forever, while murderers had a date to roam free.

CHAPTER 28

Washington, D.C.—United States Capitol Building

Hank Rudolph, fifty-two, started in law enforcement as a correctional officer at Lorton Reformatory in Lorton, Virginia. A former MPD Officer turned detective, turned US prosecutor. He had a steady sour expression and dark rings around his eyes. He looked like a man that trafficked in death. After spending over a decade working DC Homicide, he found refuge in the weight room; the man's upper body didn't appear to belong to the miserable face that sat upon it shoulders.

He had the strong body of a well-oiled tractor, with a waist that stopped of thirty-three inches and biceps that moved like boa constrictors under the arms of his form-fitting blazer.

AUSA Rudolph worked his way up through DC legal channels and had experience dismantling bombs in the military and busting narcotics rings in urban and suburban settings. He had over three hundred homicides under his belt, everything from dope dealers in the ghetto killing each other, drunk drivers taking out crowds of people in front of a bar, to the kidnapping and strangling of a local prostitute. He had held the hand of snitches as a cop and prosecutor, helping them roll over on politicians and drug traffickers, with experience on various crime task forces. He knew how to work his way through interrogations and trial because of his background in scratching the hairy underbelly of the DC criminal beast. As a prosecutor, he drove cases to convictions based on feelings formed from his cop's intuition.

That late afternoon he was in a small meeting room with a wood table surrounded by chairs, one of them bolted to the floor with shackles on the sides. David Thurman sat there, shackles locking his feet to the floor, keeping him from any attempts at escaping.

AUSA Rudolph, Captain Finnerty, and Naim Butler were perched at the table in the windowless room, preparing to get their interrogation—or interview, depending on who was asked—underway. The room wasn't big enough for all four egos.

Without a shirt on, because it had been confiscated and being analyzed, David Thurman, a behemoth man, sat there looking like he had just come off of a flat-bench, covered in sweat and military-inspired tattoos.

Pressing record on a video recorder, AUSA Rudolph said, "David Thurman, you've met Captain Finnerty, and were joined by your attorney, Naim Butler. He's an interesting man. But we're on the record now and here to get your version, David, with respect to your unlawful entry, banned display of promoting a political agenda, and your dry-run attempt to attack the United States Capitol Building."

That got a sneer from Naim Butler. "You got proof of that last charge?"

Thurman nodded his head but didn't say a word.

"We have preliminary matter to dispose of," AUSA Rudolph said, frowning condescendingly. "You're not a member of the District of Columbia bar."

Naim chuckled. "Is that how you want to start off?" he said, reaching into his briefcase. "I am, however, admitted to the New York State Bar." To support his claim, he passed the prosecutor a page printed at the Trump International Hotel's front desk. "A record from the New York State Unified Court System. Besides your position is erroneous, because I have a distinguished L.L.M. From the University of Pennsylvania School of Law, a doctor of jurisprudence from Yale. And I teach criminal law at Columbia. Moreover, Rule 49 of the Rules of the D of C allows an attorney who is a member in good standing of another bar to practice here for a period of three hundred sixty days, so long as I submit an application to the D of C Bar within ninety-days and practice under the direct supervision of a member of the D of C Bar." He passed along a confirmation that he'd submitted an application that morning, and Maria Sethmeyer was supervising him. "I believe it's your move." He smiled.

"Now you can see why I have him here," Thurman said. "He's always prepared. Guess all of that Ivy League education was worth the debt."

"I thought we'd be able to resolve this with a fair disposition," AUSA Rudolph said, "but I won't be disrespected by an outsider. Especially not an arrogant New Yorker. You know we hate New Yorkers in D.C."

"I'll ignore that in favor of sticking to the real issue," Naim replied. "Mr. Thurman is a hard sell, so anything short of us walking out of here with a warning won't sway him much."

"Yes, what he said," Thurman said, adding raised eyebrows and a head tilt.

"We need information regarding a pressing matter. Perhaps you may or may not be in a position to shed light on the matter," AUSA Rudolph said. "This morning a Supreme Court justice was viciously murdered in his home…"

"Tragedy, I know," the killer said.

"As luck would have it Americans for sentencing Reform materials that you've been handing out references two things. One, your concern over how the Supreme Court will rule on a case regarding sentencing reform set to be heard in oral argument this session. Two, how important the presidential race is this year, as the new president will likely appoint several judges considering four of them are over seventy-five-years-old."

The captain added, "Awfully coincidental of you to be making predictions and referencing matters so closely connected to the death of a prominent justice. The chief actually. If you're in possession of relevant information, evidence, or other matter regarding the death of the judge you need to turn it over."

In an attempt to stop his client from lying about the murder of the judge, he sprung into action. "What are you talking about?" Naim asked. "You're knotting this to the death of Chief Justice Weston?" A clever question to access their intelligence.

"Now that's a stretch," Thurman said and smirked. To Naim, he said, "How much of this do we got to take?"

"Not much," AUSA Rudolph said, answering for the defense attorney.

"Thanks, because the scope of that interpretation of my actions today is boring." Thurman feigned a yawn.

"Oh, we have you for serious infractions regardless," the AUSA said, layering on the possibilities of connecting Thurman's Capitol Hill action to Thurman's Georgetown actions.

"Let's cut the crap. Do you have anything linking my client to the death of anyone?" Naim asked. *More Fishing.*

"No."

"Good, then you have a summons for him to appear on that handing out materials on Capitol grounds charge?" Naim asked.

"You seem to have conveniently forgotten the illegal entry charge," Captain Finnerty said.

"It's absurd. He hasn't done that."

"Look, Mr. Butler, I'm going to give you this one courtesy, OK. In this district the unlawful entry statute is somewhat broader than its name would suggest. It covers more than merely entering onto certain premises without authority. Here to remain on property against the will of the person lawfully in charge of it is a problem," the ASUA said.

"He was asked by the US Supreme Court Police to leave their grounds, and instead of doing that, he held an interview with the media before doing so. It's really a cut and dry violation. We have it on video. Perhaps your Ivy League education doesn't equal experience and you should quit while you're ahead," Captain Finnerty said, smiling. "I guess your supervisor, Sethmeyer, isn't supervising you after all."

Despite some air being let out of his tire, Naim was stoically in his seat mentally preparing for fixing this problem. He dug into his briefcase and pulled out a leather-bound black calendar. He opened it to August, prepared to pencil in a date to appear before a US magistrate judge to have his client enter a plea of not guilty. He planned to have the matter pan out to nothing more than a warning not to violate said DC laws again. Although, he wasn't sure that would be possible for Thurman, a man set on alerting the world to his cause. And wanted for murdering four men.

"I'm going to shoot straight," AUSA Rudolph said. "We really don't like to deal with this sort of thing on Capitol Hill. There's a forum, an appropriate way to do this. Contact senators for meetings. Buy lobbyist. And other things. We can't have people distributing propaganda in the Crypt area of this building. Costumes and performers belong on a stage." He pulled out a piece of paper and slid it to Naim. "We're willing to have your client sign a contract to stay off the grounds of the Supreme Court and Capitol Hill for one- year in exchange for not pursuing this matter in federal court."

Naim made a face, an inventory clerk inspecting the goods, looking to cut out of the building. It was a standard judicial document with a direct order for Thurman to essentially stand down, silencing him in D.C. This helped him avoid a lengthy court proceeding and the tedious exchange of motions and discovery. He looked at his client who nodded in agreement to sign the form to get his show on the road. Naim knew that in D.C. there were disparate forms of evidence passed over in discovery, and scholarly court lectures by experts could derail a well-planned defense. The mere presentation to a jury that Thurman wore a costume on Capitol Hill mirroring a suicide bomb vest and used to test the response of CHPO practically promised a conviction and wasn't worth the manpower needed to defend the indictment. He simply wanted to sign the document, moving on to the case that really had him in Washington D.C. Namely, defending, David Thurman, against capital murder charges.

CHAPTER 29

Washington, D.C.

Naim walked out of the Capitol Building with Thurman by his side dressed in a T-shirt from the Capitol's gift shop.

An excellent magician was a man that excelled in the art of misdirection. The same was true for lawyers. Attorneys used sarcasm and feigned naivety to distract local authorities. They thought they'd trapped him in a hard to reach place, but they had no idea what he planned to pull from his other sleeve now that he'd gotten his client out of one jam as a more murderous one loomed.

Out on East Capitol Street, attorney and client were quiet, and it remained that way until they reached the Library of Congress. Naim wondered if they were being followed, flagged down a taxi that scooped them up. Inside the cab, Naim had the driver head to Sixth Street and Independence Avenue. Eight blocks later they exited the cab in front of the National Air Space Museum and hustled inside.

"Why are we here?" The killer asked, breaking his silence.

"The food court. It's the best in town."

"You're hilarious," Thurman said, walking through security. "I'm not into comedy." His face was deadly serious.

"OK," Naim said and stopped. He looked around the entry of the museum at the huge missile on exhibit. "We may be followed and we need to rocket up out of DC without detection. We're going to hit a side door, skedaddle to the National Mall, then hop on the local Metro train at the National Mall Station. We'll get off at L'Enfant Square. Exit. And Brandy will be there to grab us." He started to walk away, but Thurman stood there. He pointed and walked back towards his client. "You got a better idea?"

"I can handle myself from L'Enfant. I have a local hideout."

"Do you now? My plan is better."

"It's not."

"You haven't even heard it."

"I've gotten this far."

"Not going back and forth with you."

"Good. Let's go."

"I'm getting you out of DC, and someplace safe in friendly, Maryland. We can get to Potomac Airfield quickly from there. We will then craft a plan to get you safely to the authorities to take care of that other issue." Naim blinked uncontrollably. He did that when in deep thought.

"Not happening. I have a safe place here. It is absurd to leave this area. They expect that. I'm going to hide right under their noses before I bring that wasteful US attorney to full froth. In the meantime, it's PCP and cheap prostitutes. You got a problem with?"

"Listen here, you son-of-a-bitch. This is not your show, it's mine."

"Since when?"

"Since you called for my services. Let me say this in a way that you can comprehend. I'm assuming director duties."

"Have a good day," Thurman said, walking away, throwing the peace sign over his back. He had paid for Naim's services and like many defendants labored under the delusion that made him the boss. "I'll be in touch."

"Wait!"

Thurman stopped.

Grin on the murderer's face, ten to one, he contemplated strangling his attorney as he turned around. "Don't be a hero."

"Oh, I'm not. And I don't make threats. I want you to know that people who don't listen to me go to jail. For you, I'm sure the prosecutor will bake you a vicious cake."

"Ah. The scent of flesh burning on the electric chair. Mouthwatering," he replied, walking away.

————————

At the pavement, Thurman made a sweeping right passing several food carts. He bought a water from one of them, before walking at a fast pace in the direction away from the U.S. Capitol. If his lawyer had made any sense he had to take advantage of his head start. There were no witnesses to his murders, but he knew that there was an aggressive manhunt to find him.

Passing the National Museum of African Art, Thurman's cell phone chimed. The caller ID read: Unavailable. A call from his wife was right on time. He needed consoling and motivation: she would deliver both.

CHAPTER 30

Washington, D.C.—L'Enfant Square

Naim continued to process the falling out with Thurman around his mind, as he popped out the L'Enfant Plaza green-line Metro Station. The station and square were named agent French engineer, Pierre Charles L'Enfant, the man that planned the city.

The youthful-looking sex-siren, Brandy Scott, leaned on the side of the armored Escalade leaving the driver behind the wheel; no doubt, prepared to take off just in case Naim bolted from underground being followed by federal agents.

After giving Brandy a quick hug, they climbed into the back seats of the truck. The driver sped away from the curb as soon as the doors slammed shut. Settled into their seats they looked at one another.

"And where's your client, counselor? My source."

"Gone." Somber. "Where exactly are we headed?"

"Slight change of plans," she replied, smiling. "Cute pivot, though," she added, "you're becoming one ol' Washingtonian. But you're not getting off that easily. Where's Thurman?"

Staring out of the window, watching D.C fly by, he said, "He's on his own. Didn't like my plan." He snuggled up to her, resting his head on her shoulder. She draped an arm around him caressed his shoulder, while listening to his version of what had transpired between him and David Thurman over the past few hours. "I mean, if he wasn't lying, he told me graphic details about the justice's murder. The jury will be delightfully horrified."

"How'd you manage to talk at the Capitol?"

"We whispered and I had him write things down," he said, tapping his briefcase. "The notes may be leaked to a certain *New York Times* editor."

"This case will definitely have a gag order in place," she said, "so be sure they end up in said editor's E-mail inbox soon. Anonymously."

"Indeed."

"He'll be back around. He loves or likes to appear in control. A true narcissist."

"And that pisses me off. Why on earth do defendant's believe that they're in control as if they have the law degree and experience?"

"Good question, one that can be answered when we get to the Georgetown Law School. I've gotten us visitors clearance to do some legal research."

Naim lifted his head. They were being driven east on Maryland Avenue with the U.S. Capitol Building ahead, it's bronze Statue of Freedom on top looking Naim in the eye. He looked out of the back window and saw the Washington Monument in the distance, the tapering obelisk of white marble reaching five hundred fifty-five feet in the air. Panicked, he shot up, tapped the driver's shoulder, and asked, "Isn't Georgetown in the opposite direction?"

"Well, yes, it is," the driver said. "But the Georgetown University Law Center is located on New Jersey Avenue in the Judiciary Square neighborhood of the city."

Naim looked at Brandy for confirmation, as they passed the Capitol Reflecting Pool.

"I was just as perplexed," she shrugged. "But it's a strategic location on the school's part."

The lawyer sat back in his seat. His hand had a slight shake, his heart raced. He suddenly acknowledged the anxiety associated with being an attorney.

CHAPTER 31

Judiciary Square, Washington, D.C.—Georgetown Law Center

Established in 1870, Georgetown University Law School was the second largest law school in the United States and received the most full-time applications per year. The school had been moved away from the main campus to Judiciary Square, a neighborhood in Northwest Washington D.C. The area was heavily occupied by various federal and municipal courthouses and office buildings. The center of the neighborhood housed an actual plaza named Judiciary Square, and was serviced by the Red Line of the Washington Metro. They drove past the District of

Columbia City Hall and the Federal Bureau of Investigation Washington field office, before parking in the front of the Georgetown University Law Center.

Entering the library's lobby, Brandy and Naim, approached a security desk, stated their business and was directed to an administrative office. A library clerk verified their permission to enter the library and took their photo before providing them with plastic IDs with the word TEMPORARY on it.

Brandy Scott sat in the law library at a computer station logged into the Lexis-Nexis electronic law library system. Her boyfriend, the lawyer, was beside her on his own computer on his second cup of coffee. Their equal pursuit of justice provided fertilizer for their relationship to grow. There was no shouting or violence between them, just an underlying knowledge that they loved each other more today than they did the day before. Brandy was wrapped up in her work, researching the procedural history leading to Jullian Thurman's continued imprisonment. Naim was obsessed with studying the Federal Rules of Criminal Procedure as it pertained to the capital murder of a Supreme Court justice. Despite David Thurman's pissy attitude, Naim patiently awaited his call as promised. Divorce from the murder trial of the decade wasn't in the cards. Naim wasn't the kind of person who'd quit something so paramount to his branding easily.

The newspaper editor and lawyer looked over at each other, smiled, both agog over their effort to do their jobs while offering their partner smiles of confidence. They were determined to prove their willingness to meet each other halfway. Naim was proving to be a polished, flawed man, who had cleaned up his act. What he'd been through and his strength to get to where he was, had not been lost on her. Things was easy for them and she believed they'd stay that way. He was turned on by watching her avariciously devour the law. He was also turned on by the fact that she was a good-looking, brilliant woman who made him happy. She was a news editor who had a very flexible schedule, a boon for him.

They were seriously dating without any negatives. He was determined to assure that no complaining started. All of Naim's life he'd been getting the raw end of the deal and finally things were bright and optimistic.

"You know," he said, "I'm not sure if that monster is out killing right now. That's a sickening visual."

"You don't say," Brandy replied. "And he has a good reason. At least from his own twisted, demonic perspective. His wife really had a hard time in the courts. The bulk of her sentence was not for her conduct, but the conduct of the conspirators. Many of whom she didn't even know."

"How so?" he asked, pushing back in his seat, looking at her screen.

"Federal law disparately treats equal weights of powder and crack cocaine, that you know."

"I do. Whites use powder, blacks use crack and really affects the lives of black families sending dealers away for absurd mandatory minimums. Some for life. For crying out loud there are murderer's that don't get life." His voice was passionately rising.

"I hear you, but the opposition will say that dealers subject addicts to a lifetime of addiction and misery, which is cruel and unusual punishment, so life for a drug dealer doesn't seem odd. Or violate the Eighth Amendment."

"True, but this topic has reached the Supreme Court and has been debated in Congress. The disparity is unwarranted between powder and crack. Cocaine remains cocaine even in a dress and pumps."

She batted her eyes and stared at him. A blank sneer crept onto her face.

"What?" he asked, smiling conspiratorially.

"Something just dawned on me," she replied, clicking the mouse, and searching again.

"What?" he asked, inching closer to her. He dropped his arm around her shoulders.

"Despite reaching the Supreme Court the disparity hasn't been struck down as unconstitutional. And, do you know why, counselor?"

"Nope, but I'm sure you're going to school me."

"I am. Three words: Chief Justice Weston," she said, pointing at the screen.

Naim's shoulders sagged. "Weston and the liberals blocked the ratio between crack and cocaine being one to one."

"A move that would have drastically reduced the sentences of people sentenced for possessing crack. Including one, Jillian Turman."

"You should be a lawyer."

"No," Brandy said, "I should be in the business of informing the people of what they're up against."

"And, let me guess…You plan to do that?"

She kissed his lips, and said, "How'd you guess?"

CHAPTER 32

By eight-thirty, Naim and Brandy, we're having dinner at BLT Prime by David Burke, the Trump International Hotel's high-priced steakhouse, prominently located on the mezzanine. The spot overlooked the iconic Clock Tower, Naim continued to hope that no one was scheduled to die in Washington, D.C. at the hands of David Thurman, as he sipped Pinot Noir. Prayerfully, Thurman was taking a break from picking off politicians determined to keep up the war on drugs. Blocking the anxiety of more potential murders, Naim had treated himself to an in-house masseuse, facial, and manicure upon return from the law school. Over those three hours, Brandy was holed up in the suite penning a serious speculative op-ed set to be featured in the *Washington Post* and *New York Times*. The piece tied Weston's murder to his rigorous opposition to reforming drug laws. It was chock full of facts, statistics, and conspiracy theories, the kind of deliciousness that drove newspapers print sales through the roof.

While they ate, a dozen white roses were delivered to the table for Brandy. Naim had ordered them. A slice of his charm, thanking her for being a great partner in and out of bed. The gesture applauded her forcing a smile to spread on her lovely face.

"You know, you're truly amazing, but very genuine," she said smiling. "Thank you".

"What ever do you mean?" He was laughing, flashing bright white teeth.

"If I didn't know any better, I'd think you are trying to wine and dine me to get into my LaPearla's."

"Well, I am." He winked dramatically. "That's why I bought 'em."

She slapped his arm, and then said, "What I meant was, when you go out of your way to send flowers my way or other gifts, I take the gestures as your commitment to continuing to make me happy. You truly embody the spirit of happy wife-happy life. And we're not even married."

Naim simply smiled and thanked her. "For me, it's no easy task to please a woman who has it all. The one thing you can't give yourself, though, I do. I will always go out of my way to provide you with love. I mean, how else do people reach their gold anniversary?"

"Gold. I'm not sure I have fifty years left."

"But just in case you do," he said, smiling and raising his glass. "Let's toast to that."

She tapped her wine flute against his, and said, "You're really giving it your all for Happiness Happens Month."

"We could skip this and get to something else celebrated this month."

"What's that?"

"Tell me, it's National Toddler Month," he replied, smiling.

CHAPTER 33

Congress Heights, Southeast, Washington, D.C.—Forest Ridge and The Vistas Apartments

Just after midnight was really off the chain, psychotic, plain nuts. *These sad, miserable, sons-of-crack-whores are a piece-of work.* The killer wanted to shake things up again, right in the heart of the ghetto. *Right now!* Even at this hour there were far more men hanging out on the block than he cared to see. *What a bunch of losers. I can spray them all pretty quickly.*

He has watched them from three-stories up; some of them the father and mother of children who were set to travel right down their path to nowhere. Well except, jail. He thought of his own father, the absolutely irresponsible prick.

Then, he saw the tall buff drug dealer he'd been buying from, wave at an addict, pulling on his white gloves. Latex gloves were commonly worn by individuals who distributed PCP. Worthless trash. Phony salesman-like attitude written all over the dealer's face.

Boom! Boom!

Two bull's eyes.

Two exploding heads cantaloupes.

That's how their lives should end. Strong executions.

He had to block out the rude thoughts in his mind. He already had plans to take out a more important D.C. Metro-area denizen. A U.S. Senator. Maybe *dos*. They were dead meat.

The really interesting thing about the dealers was that none of them paid much attention to a pole-mounted MPD surveillance camera that captured all of their stoop sales. Thurman, with his apartment window open had previously heard the stupid ingrates express the position that the cameras were fake or inoperable.

After all, they engaged in several urban warfare-style shoot-outs and the police never showed up. He knew they were off-base. The MPD had been wearing velvet gloves with steel fists inside, undoubtedly, prepared to lay the hammer down.

David Thurman's attention was captured by an unmarked Yukon Denali rolling into the apartment complex's parking lot. Pulling out his binoculars, he smiled oddly at a team of Gun Recovery Unit officers, wearing menacing tactical gear. The apartments' residents scattered as officers exited the SUV. Officer Katz accosted Rudy Briscoe, an eighteen-year-old talking on his cell phone. Briscoe, a resident of the complex for ten years, was known to the officers and always suspected of committing one crime or another. He backed away from law enforcement, who said, "Get against the wall. You have any weapons?"

Ah, the inherent power of the unconstitutional stop and frisk tactic.

Bristol did not answer and quickened his pace. What happened next was captured on the MPD surveillance camera.

Bristol sprinted out of the parking lot into an adjacent street. Officer Katz gave chase but did not demand the suspect to stop. Officer Sheehan raced back to the Denali, hopped inside, and chased behind Briscoe without activating the vehicle's siren. They didn't want to alert any law-abiding citizens of their potential debauchery.

Crossing the street, a dark object appeared in Briscoe's right hand prompting officer Katz to snatch his weapon from its holster. Reaching the opposite sidewalk, Briscoe glanced at least twice over his left shoulder at the approaching vehicle, arms pumping, trying to reach the driveway leading to a wooded area. As Briscoe pivoted to turn into the driveway he abandoned his weapon. Continuing to flee, the Denali pulled parallel to him. Officer Sheehan pointed his gun, fired twice, hitting Briscoe in the left buttock.

Rising, falling, then, sprawling on the ground, Briscoe held his hands away from his body. Officer Katz stood over him with his gun pointed at him.

Briscoe volunteered, "The gun ain't real, please don't kill me."

CHAPTER 34

Washington D.C.—Tidal Basin

Naim Butler passed through tunnels of petals from Japanese cherry trees during his two-mile jog through the paved loop in West Potomac Park. He zipped past monuments that were lit, stunning, and inspiring his five-thirty a.m. A breath of fresh air. His curiosity about what would happen next in the Thurman saga kept him from sleeping.

You like the tension and difficulty, don't you, counselor? In fact you like it a lot? Go on. Admit it. No matter how controversial or absurd, Naim needed the killer. *What the hell are you thinking? You need a killer as much as a cartoon needs one.* You should immediately apologize to yourself for blowing this morning jog on thoughts of Thurman when you have the beautiful and accomplished Brady Scott at a luxurious hotel awaiting your return.

He hadn't lost the fact that Brandy Scott was a part of the complex investigation that he worked on. That was the perfect reason to get back to her, extending this chapter of their love affair. *Why had she been forwarded pictures of the dead justice? Why had she been a witness to her "source" being shot at and arrested? Why had she been tapped to investigate the arrest and conviction of a killer's wife?*

Albeit not in exploration mode, Naim decided to walk through the Franklin Delano Roosevelt Memorial, consisting of nine bronze sculptural ensembles depicting events from the Great Depression and World War II. Naim needed to gather the mettle to be as victorious as the thirty-second president. Japan attacked Pearl Harbor during Roosevelt's fourth consecutive term in office. David Thurman's attack on America was as heinous. An act of war. An act many would suggest that he should die for. An act that the forefathers expected the Sixth Amendment to protect.

Jogging again, Naim thought, *what a dilemma*. For Naim there was no conflict with assuring Thurman's right to effective assistance of counsel. Passing the Thomas Jefferson Memorial, he thought, *that is what you wanted, right, when signing the Declaration of Independence, staring at America's third president.*

Returning to the hotel, Naim was a man with a plan. He stretched on the pavement under five United States flags blowing freely. He was just a D.C. visitor finishing a run. A run that built his mental state—a necessity to get through the day. That was his outlook. Despite having his whole life ahead of him, he had to focus on the task at hand: Wednesday.

———

Naim walked into the hotel glad that it was shimmering with lights from chandeliers. He was done with the city being cloaked in darkness-and evil. He looked forward to sunrise, as he boarded the elevator, heading to the suite. On the hotel's top floor, he removed his headphones before entering the room. Tossing the keycard onto the living room's coffee table, he went into the bedroom.

The bed was empty.

He panicked. Even if a tiny bit.

"Hey, Bran…" he called out, looking at the closed ensuite bathroom's door.

The toilet flushed. Water ran, and then, Brandy came out of the bathroom dressed in a yellow panty and bra set. A groggy and sexy frown was written on her face.

Picking up the phone, she said, "Good morning," climbing back in bed. "I'm going to order a carafe of coffee. And since super-lawyer just worked out, a protein-packed breakfast"

Stripping out of sweaty clothing, he said, "Please and thank you. Egg whites scrambled, smoked salmon, lots of turkey bacon, orange juice, bottle of Moët. I'm going to take a quick shower before breakfast in bed. You're free to join me."

"For which part."

"Both," he said, stepping out of his boxer briefs, "But if I had to choose one, I'd take the shower," he added, walking naked to the bathroom.

CHAPTER 35

Washington, D.C.—United Medical Center

The night had been long for Rudy Briscoe and it was still going strong and hard, blending right into Wednesday morning. At seven o'clock, Detective Hill arrived in his hospital room at United Medical Center where he was on his side recuperating from a gunshot wound to the ass. Looking at the detective slam a *Washington Post* on a bedside table, his mind ran quickly to understand how carrying a BB-gun could have led to being shackled to a hospital bed with policemen guarding the door. By the looks of the bags under the detective's eyes, he hadn't slept well all night, either.

Detective Hill had come to the hospital to get information on one of the known dealers that had also fled when the GRU pulled up on the scene at Forest Ridge Apartments. All of the detective's evidence pointed to the assumption that Rudy was a member of the Forest Ridge Organization. Rudy didn't even know there was a federal prosecutor determined to turn the street-level dealers from his complex into a wide-reaching drug conspiracy. Detective Hill had the pleasure to hint at that in order to transform Rudy into a confidential informant. Or else.

Without an introduction, Detective Hill said, "I know you're in a bit of pain, but we need to talk," flashing a badge. His voice was docile and low like a deep, dark secret. The detective was a lanky, but muscular man like an Abercrombie model.

"The cops shot me," Rudy said childlike. He wasn't as tough as he often portrayed around the way.

"I'm here to interview you."

"For a job." A smirk froze on his face.

"Maybe you know things. After all, someone must know who's been supplying the Forest Ridge Complex in which you live with PCP and cocaine and guns. Someone must be trained you to sell the PCP." The detective pulled an iPad from his bag, cued up a video, and showed the man in custody footage of a young man playing with a gun and selling drugs to a white man in a ball cap and shades. "That would be you and a unknown white male." He let that sink in, and then said, "but before you get there, I better ask some preliminary questions."

"Like?"

"Are you drugged from surgery?"

"No, I'm good."

"Any drinks or drugs illegally used in the last twenty-four hours?"

"Just had one stick of the best purple haze," the perp said, smiling. "That's weed in case you didn't know."

"Do you understand what's going on?"

"Nope." And then, without prompting, he added, "Can I have a lawyer?"

"All right," the detective said, stuffing the iPad back into his bag and grabbed the newspaper.

"What do you want to talk about, first?"

"Nah, man. You're—"

"No, but I don't need a lawyer."

"You. Said that you weren't coherent. You didn't understand what was going on, so I don't want to force you—"

"But I don't understand. Why are they charging me with distribution while armed? That's crazy. The gun was fake. I don't need a lawyer. Read me my rights and let's get this shit out the way. I ain't got time to keep playing, I want to get to a bail hearing."

"Well, I mean, first of all you already told me, you were under the influence of some fire purple haze."

"Yeah, I told you the truth."

"I understand. I understand." The cop then added, "So do you understand what going on around you? Do you feel coherent?"

"Are you sure you understand? I asked because in your cargo pants pocket cops found $1,180 in cash, 16.9 grams of cocaine, 4.1 grams of heroin, sixty-eight methylone tablets, about fifty ziplock bags, a small digital scale, and a measuring spoon. If it walks like a dealer, it usually is. Keep that in mind before you answer my next question. Are you willing to converse with me?"

"Yes, I understand you probably want me to snitch on someone. I understand why you're here. I understand all that."

Detective Hill then, read Rudy Briscoe his rights, and he proceeded to orally waive them.

Rudy said, "I have a question."

"What's that?"

"What up with slim on the cover of the paper?"

"He has far bigger problems than you. He's wanted for killing Chief Justice Weston. It's been all over the news. I'm sure you've heard about it."

Rudy furrowed his eyebrows. "You don't recognize him?"

"Am I supposed to?"

"You just showed me making a sale to him on your iPad," he said, pointing at the cops bag. "He's the big spender addict that just moved into my apartment."

CHAPTER 36

Washington, D.C.—Martin Luther King, Jr. Memorial

No policeman had expected to close in on the assassin so quickly. And definitely not using intelligence from a local hoodlum to nail the killer of a Supreme Court Justice. Detective McGee hadn't ever been close to figuring out where to start looking for the man in the bank video until she received a call to interrogate, Rudy Briscoe. She was glad to have gotten a handle on things before the whole mess unraveled into another death and planned her retirement celebration.

Detective McGee and her partner were less than thirty yards away from capturing David Thurman. He was headed through a one-lane street with cars parked on each side, which snaked through a park leading to the Martin Luther King Monument. *Oh, the nostalgia.* They were coming upon the *Stone of Hope*, a thirty-feet figure of Dr. King emerging from a block of granite located on the Tidal Basin between the Lincoln and Jefferson Memorial.

It was a serene picturesque set, forcing visitors to take a trip down memory lane. At a pedestrian crossing, Thurman stopped—quite the law-abiding driver. *What a psychopath.* Was he really concerned about the group of Girl Scouts dressed in full uniform bobbing across the street in front of him?

A thoughtful man.

In an unmarked BMW, Detective McGee and Detective Bald Eagle, moseyed right up behind the tattered and bruised truck. They could read the sticker above the New York plate on the rear bumper of the expedition: Make America Great Again.

Operation Hoyasclaw was underway, named for the Georgetown University Hoyas and the MPD claws prepped to pounce on the maniac. Behind the detectives were four vehicles of MPD officers. Two helicopters offered air support and backup. If they were correct, Thurman was headed to perform and spread his sentence rhetoric leaflets at MLK monument. They planned to take him down and couldn't see how he could escape. Detective Bald Eagle thought ahead about her eventual award for the murderer's capture. Everyone would be shocked at how quickly he was caught.

But there was a chance this could get bad. Deadly bad.

"We take him as soon as he parks," Detective Bald Eagle said into a walkie-talkie. She was calm and eager—quite the top cop. She needed this to go down swiftly and without any deaths. She was prepared to take Thurman out, but she needed him alive just in case he had accomplices. Everyone had to be captured and brought to justice.

"This S.O.B. should be in the death chamber in the very near future," Detective McGee said. "No way the Supreme Court will grant him any stays to allow any crafty lawyers opportunity to help him fight for his life."

Hoyasclaw was in quite the situation. He had parked and turned to the truck off.

The detectives were two of a dozen law enforcers hopping out of their car to intercept their man at an innocent location. MLK was about to abandon his non-violent ideology. Hopefully not.

Although just after seven a.m. dozens of people were taking in the moment to read some of King's memorable quotes written on the marble wall surrounding the monument. They were about to be distracted.

The quiet trip to the civil rights era morphed into utter summer insanity. First, men and women were running. Then, guns came out. The man in the Expedition had killed the Chief Justice. This was like arresting James Earl Ray all over again—no longer an uneventful trip to a DC tourist attraction.

Detective Bald Eagle was in the house. Right in the front row. She would've paid top dollar for tickets to this show.

She got to the driver's door of the truck before her partner, as a MPD officer ripped open the passenger's door. Oddly, she wanted to slap her cuffs on the killer.

David Thurman faced her. He smiled, looking right into the barrel of her gun.

He enjoyed the spectacle of his life flashing before his eyes.

At his back, he heard, "Put your hands on the steering wheel. Slowly. Any other move and you die."

Execution style!

Thurman was caught off guard. Pure astonishment spread across his face. His show was over. But this wasn't the way he'd written the final scene.

Well, he had a co-writer now.

Where had he made a mistake?

"MPD. You're under arrest for murder. Four of them. And possibly another," Detective Bald Eagle barked at Thurman.

"Ah, the lovely Detective Marissa Bald Eagle. Didn't expect to be introduced to you under such vicious terms." David Thurman kept staring at the detective. Finally he had met her. Even if informally.

She said, "Hands up and step out of the truck, asshole."

Calm and obediently, he complied.

Before his feet settled on the pavement, Detective Bald Eagle cold-cocked him. She threw a hard overhand right that landed on his chin. His back slammed against the car, before he staggered to regain his footing, she said, "Cuff this piece of shit up."

No one said a word to her. They liked the punch a lot.

It was the cops turn to run the show.

CHAPTER 37

Washington, D.C.—Trump International Hotel

Room service—a round, middle-aged, black woman with a sharp weave job—rolled a cart into the suite. A small vase with a rose sticking out was on the top and a *Washington Post* was on the corner; the paper screaming to be looked at just as much as a commercial airplane landing on Pennsylvania Avenue. The case was prominently displayed on the front cover, above the fold, including a high-resolution color shot of David Thurman. The caption read: "Murderer Sought in Supreme Court Judge's Death."

The hotel attendant handed over the bill to be signed. Naim signed it and handed it back along with twenty-dollars. Then, the attendant triple-tapped the headline with one pink painted, manicured nail, as if Naim would miss it.

"I'll never say I child of God, no matter how wrong most of their decision-making has been, he should have his dick cut off," the woman said straight up. "This is tragic, and I hope the wife survives. But the judge was a black man and always went out of his way to vote like he wasn't from the same poverty-stricken stock as most of us. I bet some people are celebrating his death. He was still a black man. Sad, but true."

"Well, good morning to you too," Naim said. He asked, "What makes you assume it's appropriate to speak to hotel guests about such a sensitive matter? Normally, religion and politics are off limits, no?"

"Mr. Butler, FYI, what separates this hotel from many others in D.C. is that we know guests if they should be known. It helps us cater to and up-sell to them. You specialize in mitigation, so surely you know of Judge Weston's horrible record as it relates to criminal justice reform with him being a black conservative, and all." And, then she was on her chipper way.

"Now that's how to start a day," Brandy said, smiling and pulling the cart deeper into the suite.

"Very much so," replied Naim, reading the article.

"Adore you going to read that crapola on an empty tank. You know you need a full stomach to handle all the lies therein."

"I am. I always read these kind of articles. I often wonder what the hell does a killer think when they read what the media has to say about them."

"I bet it's all wrong. As a certain presidential nominee keeps saying: the dishonest media spreads lies."

"And he's right. This piece is full of opinions and all wrong in relevant places." Sitting the paper aside, he said, "If not for you, I'd truly wonder if the media was as smart as they claimed to be with their Harvard degrees. The media constantly excoriates the Republican nominee, and despite their rhetoric, she beat sixteen other conservatives to be the nominee. They spew too many opinions."

"Are you getting fresh with me so early in the day?" she asked, pouring extra champagne into his mimosa. "Here," she said, handing him a champagne flute. "You're not yourself before a morning libation."

He took the flute, swallowed the contents in three gulps, and then pulled her into his arms. "So, what do I do next? My client is on the front page of your rival. Probably the lead story on CNBC and Fox News."

"Why're you asking me? Last I checked, you're the attorney."

"I am, but you're smart."

"A split second ago, the media was opinionated and overrated." She smiled. Then frowned. "I'm the media."

"Everyone but you I meant." He smiled, blinking uncontrollably.

"You're too much."

He kissed her cheek. Then, reached onto a plate, grabbed a slice of bacon, and put an end into both of their mouths. They nibbled on the bacon until their lips met. "Let's eat," he said, "I got work to do."

CHAPTER 38

Washington, D.C.—Judiciary Square

Was the D.C. Killer caught? Or not?

That was the chief concern in the Henry J. Daly Building, Metropolitan Police Headquarters, located on Indiana Avenue in Judiciary Square. The building's name was a tribute to devoted homicide sergeant, Henry J. Daly, a twenty-eight your veteran of the Metro PD who was killed November 22 1994, by an armed intruder in the building.

Detective McGee had scheduled an anticipated conference call with the day's Field Intelligence Group. On the line, she had her MPD team and the FBI, ATF, Capitol Police, Supreme Court Police—just about the whole alphabet soup.

Reporting in on the call was Shai Brown, mouthpiece for the AUSO, and Ray Pitcairn, from the Forensic Analysis Branch at the FBI lab in Quantico, Virginia.

After quickly identifying who was on the line, Detective McGee handed the call over to FBI Agent Pitcairn.

"Based on shell casing at the scene and fragments in the two vic's skull, I can conclusively affirm that one weapon was used," Agent Pitcairn told the group. Detective McGee had been told this fact hours earlier, but it was news to the other law enforcement on the call. "An unknown gun brand 9mm was used, and as we know military men used these pieces. I'm thinking our guy is or was in the military. I'd start looking at SC rulings affecting the military."

"While we have Thurman in custody, I'm betting he has a serious cache of weapons somewhere. That is, if, he's the killer and this ATM video proves such," said Raquel E. Gur, representing the cautious ATF's voice.

Detective Bald Eagle chimed in, "We have a team searching the apartment that he's been living in. Landlord says he moved-in on August first. His vehicle is being combed as we speak. We will be briefing you all before the four o'clock hour, as we're sure how thirsty the media hounds will be looking for a sound bite and we need you prepared. We're encouraging you all to respond, 'no comment.' At the bottom, we may not have the actual killer in custody or he may have accomplices, so we need to keep things very close to the chest."

"Detective McGee, Captain Finnerty, here, Capitol Police. Your reports indicate that we have a killer on the loose that's advanced, methodical, and practical. I've had direct contact with Thurman, and he doesn't come off as demonstrating any of those qualities. Perhaps he's the guinea pig. In fact, I'd venture to describe him as weak. Maybe even paranoid schizophrenic. Gravely disabled and incapable of such a high degree of precision."

"Which is why he was caught on a bank video using a victim's card," AUSA Brown said sarcastically. "Anyone can murder. Getting away is entirely different. Especially in the district. It's not all that all that easy to escape and this guy knew that; hence, the local digs avoiding checkpoint traps. Let's leave the diagnosis to doctors and possible trial strategies to defense counsel with respect to whether or not he has mental defects."

"I'm armed with a psychology degree and consult with and diagnose patients part-time at George Washington University Hospital. I am over qualified to make that supposition." *Boom!*

Detective Bald Eagle stepped in. "Captain Finnerty, please forward a summation of your observations regarding Thurman to me and AUSA Brown."

"Done," he replied.

"Perfect," Detective McGee said. "Our team is or should be, finishing up with the apartment and car. I will bring you up to speed with their findings in a special report forthwith. Included will be a recording and notes of our interrogation intelligence."

CHAPTER 39

Detective McGee offered to mention, Randy Crawford, Army's Joint Terrorism Task Force, name during her press conference in exchange for a fast turnaround to determine if David Thurman was a member of the armed forces using his CJIS connections. The fingerprint Examination Section had already concluded that Thurman didn't have any criminal record as his prints didn't match any of the tens of millions of samples in the NCIS database. That was pretty bad because criminal history often told a suspect's dark secrets, and detectives were listening.

CJIS stood for Criminal Justice Information Services, a part of the FBI based in Clarksburg, West Virginia. After a two hour wait, Detective McGee was back on the line with Randy. He had fantastic news.

"Your guys a former Army Captain, McGee. Not any other agency like FBI or Secret Service. And I hope you don't mind me being a good guy and running his name through ABIS at Defense while I was at it. He's never been detained by U.S. Forces. I hope that useful."

"Well, it narrows some things and disproves a theory or two. Thanks, Randy. Next time I'm in West Virginia—"

His chuckled cutting her off. "Stop it. I'll be in D.C. for a training at the State Department next month. Drinks and sex on you."

"I look forward to it," she said. "On your life, hun. Take care, Randy."

Her next interaction was with Detective Bald Eagle. She shared the news, such as it was.

"No worries, my dear. We're just getting started," she told her partner. "It's barely noon. We have a lot of day left."

"And you're right, Detective McGee replied, smiling. Another possibility has already wormed its way into her mind. "Were weapons found at the creep's apartment?"

"Yes."

"We need ballistics ASAP, and I want a team back at that apartment to look for the prints of anyone that's been in contact with this trash." She pushed back from her desk, and said, "Let's go have a word with him. And please be civilized."

"He killed a judge. I'll try. But he doesn't sound like the civilized type."

"Says the bad cop."

Detective Bald Eagle winked.

CHAPTER 40

McGee and Bald Eagle were headed to interview Thurman when they were accosted by James Copper from their Communications Office.

"I hate to pull you away from your investigation," he's said. "But I must. Orders from the OO."

Detective McGee looked at a wall clock—eleven forty-five. Translation: several dozen reporters were crowded on the building's steps, waiting to hound her for their noon news cycles. And they had orders from the chief to be transparent. *This is bullshit*, she thought, but *let's do this*.

Walking to the elevators to feed the animals, James ran down a few things for her to cover along the way.

"Casey Greene for CNN wants to mic you up live for Wolf Blitzer tonight."

"Not a chance," Detective McGee said. "I adore Wolf—is that his birth name—he's annoying with the repetitive questions just reworded, albeit smart. CNN has enough talking heads to break down what I plan to say. That's how's this goes. I talk. They spew interpretations. Which are typically off-base."

"And conjecture," said Bald Eagle.

"OK. And I've got the NBC World News ready to cover whatever you want."

The elevator door opened, but before they boarded, Detective Bald Eagle huffed and said, "Look, James, we're not doing anything extraordinary until we can say we charged someone. Got it?"

"Loudly," he said, "but don't whine when you want primetime coverage and they're onto the next story."

"That's your job to get us coverage," McGee reminded him.

"I'll never whine, doll," Bald Eagle said. "That's for male detective's. Make a note of it."

When they reached the ground floor, James watched the women fixing their hair in the elevator mirrors. "Pardon, Gigi Hadid and Kylie Jenner? Can you two get out of the mirror? Geesh." James was excellent at his job. The last thing he needed was them fixing their hair being the story and not the justice, especially, for a daily press briefing. They were expected to look worn not all glamourous.

The detectives were assaulted with shouts from reporters as soon as they hit the steps of the Daly Building.

"Marissa. We know you hate to talk, but what happened in Georgetown?"

"Detective McGee, over here!"

"Is Judge Weston's wife still living?"

"What about the rumor—"

"Helloooo!" James sang loudly over the posse. His voice was a brave boom that demanded order. "Let the detective's make a statement before you shout at them like you just heard the opening bell on Wall Street."

Detective McGee ran down what they should have already known. Mentioned, in case they forgot, that the investigation was ongoing. Skipped that they had a suspect in custody and weapons at ballistics. After that, it was back to the scramming brawl.

The first one that James selected to talk was a Channel 4 reporter. She looked fresh out of journalism school, and asked, "Detective McGee, do you want to tell the man you're looking for in the ATM surveillance anything?" Adding, "He may be watching you."

So why the hell do you demand cops tell you investigative detail? she thought. Everyone on the steps became quiet, they were deeply interested in her reply.

The detective looked into a camera, and said, "Why don't you come on in. We're at three hundred Indiana Avenue. If you have no idea how to get here, I can have a comfy car with red and blue lights on top to pick you up."

She didn't make a splash, or say anything that would have triggered any killers to cut loose. They'd already decided to keep the fact that they had the ATM Bandit in custody under wraps.

"Blair, Fox News," James said, pointing to another reporter, she was unable to get her questions off.

"Unnamed sources say you already have the man in custody in the surveillance video."

That was, Martin Lowe, one of the crime correspondents for the *Washington Post*. He was looking down at an iPad as if he'd just gotten word form an unnamed source on it.

"Detective McGee, is there any truth to the rumor that you picked a guy up in a SUV this morning at the MLK monument? And can you tell us if this guy was determined to kill black people? Rumor has it, he killed Judge Weston for being a black conservative jurist."

The detective wanted to commit a murder of her own. This, Martin Lowe, guy was definitely in bed with someone close to the investigation. That was his prerogative. His job. But she had directly warned everyone to keep the arrest of Thurman close to the chest. Obviously someone on the FIG conference call was going to be a problem, so even they'd be starved of certain information. To hell with the Oval Office and her chief.

She gave a wonderful reply, "No comment on that at present." That line was tantamount to throwing a sardine to a dolphin. The whole squad pressed her for more.

"Hellooo!" James said with a stiff hand in the air. "I call on you and the detective responds. You learned that in Journalism one-o-one."

It didn't matter, though, Detective McGee gave more consecutive "no comments" before they pivoted, but the damage was done. If David Thurman had accomplices, they were warned. The first leak in the case, and the Babes of D.C. policing planned to be sure there wasn't a steady drip.

CHAPTER 41

The detective had barely entered the building before they were greeted by Officer Fitzpatrick. He held a secure cell phone in Detective McGee's —the lead detective's—face.

There had been a murder in DuPont Circle.

"Detective McGee? It's Sergeant Joel Pisano from Two D. We've stumbled across a murder that seems right up your alley. Very nasty artwork. His face is quite the canvas. No Testicles."

"Who's the vic?" she asked entering the elevator, headed back to her desk.

"Senator Jacob T. Elberg, ma'am. I'm calling you because he fits right into the mold of your case. Dead security on his lawn. Wife bashed in the face and in critical condition."

Democrat, Senator Elberg, had been the ranking member on the Senate Judiciary Committee. He was well-known for stalling votes in committee that reversed the harsh drug laws drafted in the nineties. Fame came his way when his hacked E-mails revealed that he vowed to continue to clandestinely oppress black men for their migrating from urban ghettos to white suburbs, peddling crack and hard dick to innocent young white women. According to Elberg, America needed less mulatto babies, stalling the growth of the pure black population.

Another gruesome incident and another bad D.C. insider ripped right out of the headlines—Washington, we have a pattern.

Detective McGee sat at her desk, pulled out a pen and asked, "Where are you?"

"1797 New Hampshire Avenue, NW. Dupont Circ. You're familiar with this area, right?"

"Of course," she told the sergeant. Handing the address to Bald Eagle, she said, "Pull that up on Google Earth for me, please." Returning her attention to Sergeant Pisano, she said, "Has the paramedics gotten there, yet?"

"Yes ma'am. The senator was ruled dead minutes before I called you."

"So no one else is in the house?"

"Not yet. I've called D.C. Mobile Crime to get the scene processed for you."

"Any shells around to know what kinda gun was used?"

"I'm no expert, but my best guess is a semi-auto. There's a lot of casings, and from a big weapon." He chuckled. "I frequent the range and do a lot of testimony. People are killing cops nowadays."

"OK." She was looking at the corner home on Detective Bald Eagles' screen. "Set up a command post on the street—not the yard,

Sergeant. Put an officer at the front, back, and sides of the home. No one enters. No one in the driveway, either. If the neighbors are out of their homes, they're not allowed on the block. Block access as done for the home of a president. We need to check the neighbor's property for footprints and other forensics. No one in the home until I get there. I'm sure Capitol Police, FBI, ATF, hell, maybe the chief too, will be there. Tell them to call me if they don't like my rules. This is an MPD case, and I am the lead homicide detective, period."

"Anything else, ma'am?"

"Just one other and this is important, so imperative, violators will be forced into early retirement, trust. No, and, I seriously mean this, no officers are to talk to reporters. None! When they arrive they're to be ignored by everyone, but you. Tell them to wait for an official briefing. No mention that the senator is dead. Has the wife been taken to the hospital?"

"Yes. George Washington University Hospital."

"Very good. No mention of her, either. You got it?"

"I do."

CHAPTER 42

Naim had been trying to reach David Thurman, since he saw his face on the corner of the newspaper. Watching the noon news, he finally had his answer as to why he couldn't reach the murderer. He grabbed a notepad off of the end table and started scribbling notes. Capturing all of the different threads covered by the newscaster regarding Thurman's arrest had marked up the lawyers mental drawing board.

Then, he was caught by surprise.

Ladies and gentleman, start your engines.

"This afternoon, from the E. Barrett Prettyman U.S. Courthouse in Judiciary Square, an exclusive live chat with Shai Brown, the man set to prosecute Judge Weston's and Senator Elberg's killer."

On the screen, Naim saw a black prosecutor, and thought they'd assigned a black face to litigate on behalf of the United State considering David Thurman was represented by a black defense attorney. *That was cute.*

"Handsome for a prosecutor," Brandy said, igniting the spark of anger that had consumed him.

On the TV: "With the assistant United States attorney today is Judge Weston's son, Marquis Weston. Mr. Weston, everyone in America and around the world are wondering how's your mother?"

"She's currently in stable condition, after three surgeries. She's going to need facial reconstruction."

"We're sorry to hear that and send her our warmest regards," the reporter said, turning his attention to AUSA Brown. "Normally. You don't go on the record before a case as big as this one—why today?"

"Because striking details regarding this case has come to light, and I must make an appeal for Washington to be alert and vigilant." The reporter nodded, and he went on. "We do have the man in the ATM surveillance footage in custody; however, we also have a pattern brewing. I can definitively inform the public that Senator Jacob Elberg has been murdered in his home, and his wife, like Judge Weston's, was brutally assaulted but not killed. Timeline details are in question, but we're working with the possibility of a serial killer. Or a team of them."

"It's being reported that David Thurman, the man in custody has hired, recently pardoned New York attorney, Naim Butler to represent him."

"He has."

"Are you worried about that? He's a UPenn and Yale, Baker and Keefe man."

AUSA Brown snickered, "And an ex-con. He's never led any case, much less one of the death penalty kind. He's unworthy...."

"Oh, boy. How wrong you are, my fried of the court," Naim said, smiling. "Underestimating my abilities is his first loss." Picking up his cell phone he texted, Maria Sethmeyer, informing her to meet him at the B&K D.C. HQ. It was time to ratchet up the stakes for a D.C. showdown.

The reporter asked, "So you're prosecuting this as a federal crime? What about MPD investigators. Will this be a DC war?"

"No war. They're investigating. My office is prosecuting."

"How wrong you are, Mr. AUSA Shai Brown. Your little comment calling me worthless," Naim said, looking deeply into the tv screen, "was an act of war."

"Wait," Brandy said. "He didn't call you worthless."

"That's what I heard," he said, smiling. "And I *is* sticking to that, using it for fuel to crush, Mr. Shai Brown." He chuckled insanely.

CHAPTER 43

The Baker and Keefe Law firm occupied floors eight through twelve of a building on K Street. The D.C. branch of B&K had remarkable financial success, predicated on its sixty lawyers billing an average of two hundred hours a month at an average of three hundred dollars an hour, grossing an average of one hundred seventy-five million a year, and earning partners nearly two million in their coffers a year. Their group of lobbyists had power on par with Wall Street firms. Maria Sethmeyer had been a partner for two years. She snatched one-point-two million a year and was shooting to double that by fifty. She was forty-seven.

Naim was welcomed to the D.C. Office with an outstretched hand by Mariah. A tall, botox-faced, former college tennis star, Maria had three Ivy-league degrees on her decorative resume.

"As one of the New York partners, your perks here are many," she said, exiting an elevator with Naim in tow. They walked along a corridor covered in plum-colored carpeting to mask the footsteps of traffic passing offices filled with attorneys-at-work. "I have a personal secretary and two paralegals getting set to assist you. And an enormous office with windows with a peek at the crown of the Capitol Building and the Washington Monument."

"Thank you," Naim said blandly, walking into an office. He was determined and not impressed by the wood-paneled walls, the leather furniture, the glass desk, or a rug imported from Turkey on the hardwood floor. Clicking his wingtips on the mahogany, he had a seat behind the desk in a high-backed, studded-chair and then said, "I'd like to get to work. Could you send in my team as soon as they arrive, please."

"I like that. Assertive and prepared to get to work." She smiled. "Yes, you'll be fine in Washington."

"I believe so," he said, powering on the desktop computer.

"All of your New York billing codes and passwords will get you access to what you've been cleared to get into in New York. How do you take your coffee?"

"Extra. Extra," he said, tapping keys on the keyboard.

Thirty-Nine was hardly a ripe old age, but he worked harder and efficiently to easily get his morning started. Five years from now, even ten years, he wanted to splurge a rough night on the town, tack on a bit of hide-the-sausage, take it down in the wee hours, catch some fast sleep, tip out of bed at six-thirty, take a cold shower, and go whistling off to face to the day's menu, without hardship.

———————

Twenty minutes passed before there was a light rap on the door. Three people—two women and one man—walked in wearing determined smiles. All business. They stopped in front of his desk, and he stood shaking all of their hands.

One of them pushed a mug in his hand, filled coffee and added extra creamer and extra sugar.

"You must be my secretary?" Naim said to the woman who passed him the mug.

"Correct. Margaret Mason. Nice to meet you." She was something. A dazzle of delicious colors: metallic hair, cloud inspired eyes with lashes like crisp centipedes, a wide mouth with fuchsia lips, rosy cheeks. The white button-up was cinched with a belt wide enough for Air Force One to land on it. Her skirt of pink, gray, and white Burberry icon print was so tight that looking at her sideways resembled a map of Africa. Black stilettos. Purple-colored fingernails, more like Raven claws. A brilliant walking Davinci.

"I'm Daniel Watts, your paralegal. I specialize in constitutional law strategies with strong reliance on Supreme Court precedent."

The paralegal, no doubt, was a wizened black gentleman slightly younger than God. His hair and shadow beard were snow-white, matching his perfect teeth.

"And, I'm Christina Gordon, also a paralegal. I focus on D.C. law and precedents that support a specific trial strategy." He figured her for Britain blood. The accent gave it away. She was razor thin, with bronzed skin, jeffy hair, a nose that could slice turkey.

"OK, let's take seats," Naim said, sitting down. He spun his computer screen so that they could see it.

"Handsome," Margaret said, smiling.

"You realize that's a mug shot," Daniel said, sneering and shaking his head.

Naim simply smirked. "That's our client, one David Thurman. His wife is currently serving time in federal prison. Her sentence sparked the murder of Justice Weston and Senator Elberg. David, before being caught, was determined to kill every liberal legal mind who set out to keep his wife in jail for a mandatory sentence."

"Why'd he only target liberals?" asked Christina.

"I'll ask when I chat with him after his meeting."

"Sounds crazy to me," Daniel said, swiping keys on an iPad.

"You might be right," Naim replied. To Margaret: "I need a list of psychologists prepared to evaluate competency. Second, I want every morsel of data that led to the prosecution of Mrs. Thurman."

"Are we representing her too?"

"No. I just want a profile on her. Perhaps, I may need our lobbyist to brief me on what's in the works to fix her predicament. That is, if she is truly in one."

"Got it," she said fully satisfied, scribbling on a pad.

"For you two," Naim said, "I want extensive details about the statutes David could possibly be charged with." He handed them a one page summary of what he knew David had done. "I need to know every possibility. The Feds are notorious for holding back charges to use during plea negotiations as a threat for a superseding indictment. Investigate all of his priors, if he has any, so we can determine sentencing exposure. I don't want the AUSA dictating my playbook. I want to control using all offense."

"Funny you should mention that. I, as instructed by Maria, sent a courtesy Email over to Shai…" said Margaret.

"Who happens to be the Chief of the Criminal Division; ergo, they've brought out the big guns," Daniel said, cutting into her statement.

"…informing him that you were taking the case and that no one in law enforcement with any agency is to speak to David Thurman without you being present. He swiftly replied, indicating that he wanted to meet ASAP to interrogate, Thurman, and to discuss options for moving forward that do not result in increased exposure for Thurman."

"Odd," Christina said, "because he'll likely be charged with 1111, first-degree murder. Not many options to increase exposure when you're starting at a mandatory life or the death penalty."

CHAPTER 44

Washington, D.C.—DuPont Circle

The press was going mad when Detective McGee arrived in swanky DuPont Circle. *Good for them.* DuPont Circle is a traffic circle, park, neighborhood, and historic district in the Northwest quadrant of the city. The area was named for Rear Admiral Samuel Francis DuPont. The neighborhood declined after World War II and vastly during the 1968 riots. Fueled by urban pioneers the area enjoyed a resurgence during 1970s, taking on a bohemian feel and becoming popular among the gay and lesbian community. Lambda Rising, D.C.'s first gay bookstore opened there in 1974 and gained notoriety in 1975 when the store ran the world's first gay-oriented television commercial. Tons of cameras fought for a shot of Jacob and Lisa-Marie Elberg's glass and marble house, either out front behind the barrier set up by Sergeant Pisano, or around the corner on the side where the policeman had camped out to keep reporters out because they undoubtedly would attempt to enter.

She looked at the other homes on the block as she pulled up, and saw neighbors watch the live show. She parked, checked in with crime-scene attendance, and immediately ordered a canvassing detail to start interviewing the looky-loos on the set. Detective Bald Eagle was by her side quietly taking visual photos of the area. She was good at that.

Entering the home, they started in the den, where the Elberg's had been playing scrabble—the board was still between them, unmolested. Their TV—wall mounted and above a chimney—was on NBC Channel 4 with a live angle outside the home.

"They're out of line," Sergeant Pisano said. "The press loves to cry about peoples' privacy but they always violate the rights of victims."

The den hadn't been disturbed, except for the blood littered here, there, and everywhere. Sergeant Pisano had relayed that he surmised the killer had the couple at gunpoint as soon as he greeted them. Senator Elberg's hands were handcuffed. His hands were left positioned as if in prayer.

Senator Elberg was casually perched in his recliner. In death, he looked most excellent. The single slash crossing his mouth looked pristine, with a purple-ish ring surrounding it. *The Joker, perhaps?* Detective Bald Eagle put her face close to the wound.

"It's safe to say he'll no longer be shouting on the Senate floor anymore," Detective McGee said, pointing at the smile extension. "Cut in the mouth and stabbed in the right parietal." She pointed at a set of French doors, leading to the patio. "And that's where our killer came on in, I'd bet."

The brick patio had a stone fireplace and narrow walkway leading to a yard and a two car garage. Four trees with apples and oranges growing from branches lit-up the space.

Beyond that, the side of the neighbor's three-story Victorian cast an eerie shadow over the detective's when they stepped onto the patio.

"Were the neighbors home?" Detective Bald Eagle asked.

"They were. The Donahue's. Husband and wife didn't see a thing and didn't hear any shots. They…rather the husband, noticed the dead security detail on the front porch when he let their collie out to poop. Seems your guy walked right up to the front door," Sergeant Pisano said, poking a hole in the idea that the killer entered through the patio.

"Assuming this is our guy," Detective McGee said.

"It's the guy," her partner replied.

"Pardon me, Detective?" A MPD officer was suddenly behind them. He held up gloved hands. "Two things, Detectives, Sarge. Neighbors say a beat up Expedition has been parked on the block. One person distinctly recalls the SUV having New York Plates. Another family across the street noticed it, took pictures of it and the driver, and called police to have it looked into. I've asked them to gather all of their surveillance for us to view."

This wasn't the kind of purlieu where *beat-up* trucks were en vogue, Detective Bald Eagle made a note to follow-up, but she had just captured, David Thurman, in an Expedition with New York plates. *Coincidence? Or, no?*

"And the other thing?"

"The fantastic FBI has arrived."

"Have them send their Emergency Response Team around the driveway," Sergeant Pisano said.

"Oh, it's not ERT, sir. It's an *agent*. He asked for Detective McGee."

Leering back inside, she watched a white guy with shoulder-length brown hair and aviator shades masking his eyes in a standard FBI polo shirt. He wore latex gloves, peering at the hole in Senator Elberg's head.

"Back up," Detective McGee called through the patio door. "Why the hell are you here?"

To be nice, he ignored her.

"Did he give a name?"

"Morgan, ma'am."

"Hey, asshole," she shouted this time and then started inside.

"Don't touch a damn thing in there."

When she reached the den, Morgan stood straight up and looked deep into her eyes. *Nice piece of ass,* Morgan thought and smiled extending his hand.

"Alexander Morgan. Washington field office. Pleasure is all mine."

Detective McGee shook the man's hand respectfully, but it was an electrifying moment, like the NFL game kick off. And we're underway.

"What are you doing here." Detective Bald Eagle wanted to know.

"Getting a head start on the investigation," Morgan told her, smiling.

"You're shitten me. You don't have any reason to be concerned with this body."

He looked at her and grinned. "I have specific POTUS orders to be here." Knowing that little factoid, he did exactly what the MPD wouldn't expect. He gave them his back and continued to analyze the senator. The corpse.

Clean shot and a cleaner—more precise—slit throat. A very clean getaway. Complete expert action. So effective. So deadly. He found the killer to be a worthy adversary.

Into a recorder, he said, "Ballistics results ASAP. But this looks like a 9mm. I bet this guy had military training. The throat precisely opened giving it away. Maybe military medical training. We're looking for a rogue trader. Straight Benedict Arnold."

"You must have had access to my initial report?" Detective McGee asked.

"Wow, you question my competence and experience without knowing a thing about me. Smart." He stood up, and said, "See, that's why I'm here."

"Look, you're not needed. You're voicing what we know. Just an arrogant Bureau ass with an inflated perception of entitlement," Detective Bald Eagle said.

"Cute," Morgan said. "I don't care about credit for this. The U.S. attorney, Shai Brown, will get all of the accolades for knocking this out of the park, right?"

"Man, we don't have time for your federal gloating." That was Sergeant Pisano.

Finally, the man before him opened his mouth. *Time to work.* The FBI Agent stepped into Sergeant Pisano's face. *Close.* "You got the D.C. game fucked up," FBI Agent Morgan said, letting the politeness seep out of his introduction. *Closer.* He had been a nice, little federal agent, allowing them to pop verbal shots at him. Now it was his turn. *Too close for comfort.* "See this murder and the last four over in Georgetown occurred in my district, making it a federal crime, which I happen to investigate and bring perpetrators to justice. Be nice or I can have this home taken over as my very own man-made island, and you'll immediately be deported.

CHAPTER 45

No doubt, when Naim Butler, Esq., arrived at the Henry J. Daly Building on Indiana Avenue shortly after four that afternoon, he had no idea who Henry J. Daly was or why the nation's police headquarters was named after him. He did have an idea, though he didn't want to be at Henry's and, all he wanted was to chat with his client and get out of there. He exited the elevator in the basement, assuming a cell block was there with his client locked in a cell. He passed through the metal detector and had his briefcase searched. Sitting at a worn desk was a slim wench. No more than twenty-five, Naim imagined.

"Naim Butler to see David Thurman."

"You the lawyer?" She was the look-at-me-bitch type: so brunette, so top-heavy, so bright, so addictive that he stood up straight, poking out his chest.

Vanity, they name is man.

She was pecking away at an old phone, the tip of a pink tongue slipped from the corner of her full mouth.

I'd trade my Benz for one—Enough, he thought. *That way lied the end of your well-being.*

"Yes ma'am, I am the lawyer."

After speaking into the telephone receiver, she frowned at him. "It seems that he's not allowed visitors by anyone." She gave that "anyone" the husky, Marilyn Monroe exhalation, arching her back, pouting.

Lord help me.

"I'm his attorney, not anyone. Who were you speaking with?" He didn't let his brewing disbelief show.

"AUSA Brown."

"Can you be so kind to get him on the line, again."

"No, I cannot."

His anger was simmering, but he remained calm. Partly because he needed to demonstrate humility, but mostly, he couldn't yell at the lovely cop. "Ma'am, I think I told you that I am, David Thurman's attorney. To block me from seeing him would be a gross violation of his constitutional rights. My cell phone is in my car or I'd call Brown myself."

"Then go to your car. It's really that simple."

"Look—" Naim began.

"Mr. Butler?" Someone called at his back. "Shai Brown, assistant United Stated attorney. Nice to meet you. Finally. I've read so much about you."

"All lies I'm sure."

He furrowed his brows. "Come with me a second."

Naim stood there. "Am I going to be able to see my client, David Thurman?"

"Of course, I wouldn't infringe on his rights. But let's get out of this corridor. We have somethings to cover."

"Before we cover your things, I need to speak with my client. There's no way, I would communicate anything of value to you without a talk with Mr. Thurman."

"Sounds fair. And I'll allow it—"

"You don't have much of a choice."

And let the pissing contest begin.

"But be sure to inform him this fact: Pleading guilty is his only decision necessary to avoid a trip to being one of the select few to experience being housed on the death unit at USP Terre Haute."

"Wrong! His best decision for avoiding any Con Air trip to Indiana was hiring me."

CHAPTER 46

Having decided to ignore Agent Morgan's absurdity, Detective McGee pulled Sergeant Pisano back and politely informed the federal pig that he could threaten them, but she knew he couldn't kick the MPD off the case no more than she could him. It was really a moot point to make. Working in tandem to solve the crimes that he gripped their city was far more important than measuring who had the bigger political phallus.

Walking outside of the Elberg house about a half-hour later a whole throng of the press was being fed by FBI Agent Morgan. Detective McGee made a beeline towards him.

"We are undoubtedly looking into ties between Chief Judge Weston and Senator Elberg," the agent had said.

"Excuse me, Agent Morgan?" Detective McGee called over the reporter's shouts. "Can I have a word with you, sir?"

He nodded, turning back to the press corps.

She said, "Now," rocking back on her heels.

Agent Morgan produced a wide smile. "Of course," he said.

"Pardon me, ladies and gents."

Together they walked towards the house to put distance between them and the media.

"What now, Detective McGee?" he said, stopping.

In a whisper, because she had no idea how far the presses microphones could pick up sound, "You need to carefully vet who, if any reporters you talk too."

"Are you telling me how to do my job?" he said. "I'm not getting you."

"You get me. You've been in Washington long enough. Don't give me that dumbfounded mug. Certainly, I had your bio and resume sent to me. No way was I working with some amateur on this. I know most of those clowns over there. Jack Moore is from the Post and he badly wants a spot in a comfy chair on the set of Good Morning D.C., but he lacks the talent and the face. He smears our department with force. The cute black one is Brandy whatshername from New York. She's with the Times, and guess what, the only reason she's here is because the man, David Thurman, that we have in custody is represented by her boy toy. There's already been a leak. We cannot afford one that will drip right into the hands of defense counsel."

He looked at her as if she was speaking-in-tongues at a church deep in Tennessee.

"Please tell me your department had nothing to do with the media finding out that we had Thurman in custody?"

"We didn't," he said, stepping back, "and don't be accusing—"

"Man, shut the fuck up," Detective Bald Eagle said. "I've had it up to here,"—she bent down and held her hand just above her ankle—"with you. Any higher and I'm going to forget which side you're on."

"You two are a really good tandem." He smirked.

"Look, the last thing any of us needs is to be seen beefing outside of a dead senator's home with the media recording our every hand gesture, our body language, and possibly recording our faces to later try to read our lips," Detective McGee said. Turning to face Agent Morgan, she said, "We don't need misinformation or any information spreading wildly thanks to those dishonest assholes. Just please let us stick to the daily press briefings, where we carefully feed the media what we want the public to know."

CHAPTER 47

Washington, DC—The Daly Building

Naim waited in a crappy room, bare except for the standard carved up wood table and two battered wood chairs. He sat, staring at the beige walls until David Thurman was let in, bringing along with him a foul body odor like a thick layer of icing on a cake. He looked his attorney up and downsizing him up, maybe?—covered his mouth with a fisted hand and sneezed violently several times. Then he said, "So glad you came."

On the contrary, I'm not thrilled. "Duty calls," Naim replied.

David Thurman was forty-six, appeared much younger, but he looked weak and tired. He was a tall man with wide shoulders. His usually neat hair was a mess; it was red, hung right over his ears, and appeared wet, obviously from sweat. His eyes were milky ovals with big blue centers, but they seemed vacant. He had to be attractive at some point in his life. Today wasn't a reflection of it.

Naim was wearing his glasses that late afternoon; he cared if people thought that he looked smart enough to be a lawyer. He didn't shake Thurman's hand or give him a fist bump even though he always shook hands with clients. He learned long ago shaking hands with new clients was *code* for trustworthiness and forthrightness, thus making the client more apt to pay bills without questions. Thurman looked like he'd pass along a communicable virus, so touching was out the window. Naim signaled for him to sit down. He didn't. He paced.

He walked five steps and did an about-face. Five more steps and another about-face. He rubbed his arms as if the warm room was frigid. His legs were wobbly and twitched uncontrollably. Halfway into his five-step walk, he doubled over and roared like he had just mustered the strength to squat one thousand pounds.

"Are you OK?"

"Withdrawal."

Like many men and women who abstained from drug abuse, Naim wanted to admonish his client and question why not get into rehab and off that stuff. It was much easier to suggest to them to understand the psychological addictive nature of drugs. Knowing that, Naim nodded to avoid being condescending.

A few minutes passed, Thurman stood straight up and began pacing again. Apparently, the withdrawal had subsided. After two passbys, he stopped, pulled out a chair, copped a squat, staring at his counselor. The dark rings around his eyes and dry lips were magnified.

"Why are you here?" Thurman asked. He looked perplexed. Bewildered.

"Because you hired me to represent you." Naim had no desire to josh with the killer before him. He preferred to be in his comfy home office, doing what he liked most: sentencing mitigation. He had fully appreciated that as a lawyer he had to prevent people from even getting to the sentencing phase of the judicial process.

David cocked his head to the side, furrowed his brows—practically making them meet at the bridge of his nose—before he said, "Who the hell are you?"

Naim snatched off his glasses, "Come again."

"Are you some kind of sexual predator?" Thurman asked, pushing back in his chair, frowning indignantly.

"What?"

"I will not come again, or at all, perv. Who the hell are you? Where are we? Why am I trapped in this room?" He stood aggressively.

Naim stood, watching the menacing flare envelope David Thurman's demeanor. Thurman backed into the corner, before dropping to his knees. He bowed his head, leaving his eyes open staring up at Naim child-like now. His hands met, and then he prayed, "Jesus, help me. Oh God, have mercy on me. Please don't let this man hurt me this evening. God, please…No…No…No. Please, in the name of the Father, The Son, and The Holy Ghost. Amen. Amen. Amen."

Naim and Thurman's eyes remained locked before Thurman closed his eyes and a wide smile spread across his face. After he recovered, he stood, took a seat at the table and tented his hands on his lap. He lightly rocked, shaking his head.

Retaking his seat, Naim dug into his wallet, retrieved a business card and slid it across the table to Thurman. He picked up the business card with his thumb and forefinger and held it before his face.

"You an ESQ?"

"Yes, a lawyer."

"You a lawyer?" He massaged his temples. Tossing the card into the air, he said, "Then, tell me, Mr. Lawyer. Why am I here?"

"OK, I'll play along," Naim said. *Somebody help me.* "You're accused of killing a judge, a senator, a judge's clerk, four U.S. Marshals. Attempted murder and assaulting two wives." He ticked off each of the deceased with a finger. Holding up nine fingers, he then extended a tenth and said, "And, use of a weapon to commit said crimes of violence."

"No way."

"Yes way."

"Hell-to-the-no." The murderer shook his head. His eyes become watery. "I'd remember that."

"Selective memory. Look, I don't have time or energy to exert on this charade…"

"I want my daddy." He stomped his feet.

What the fuck. "Excuse me."

"I want my daddy. Please," Thurman said, folding his arms across his chest, sounding like a ten-year-old. A lone tear escaped his right eye. "Dad help me. I promise to be good."

"I don't know what you're doing, but…"

"Why are you yelling at me?" More tears materialized. "I'm telling my father."

Naim stared blandly. He was never lost for words. This qualified as one.

"I want to go home," Thurman said, sniffling and hugging himself. "Can I go home?"

"You're under arrest."

"OK, I'll play along," Thurman said, mimicking the lawyer, "I'm a kid. The cops don't lock up kids. I know that much."

Naim stood up, grabbing his briefcase. At the room's door, he said, "I'll be back," sounding more like the Terminator than he wanted.

"Mr. Lawyer," Thurman called through tears, stopping Naim's exit. Looking Naim in the eyes, a broad, wicked grin spread across his face. "Have Brandy get the three-inch, bold headline ready: **NOT GUILTY BY REASON OF INSANITY**."

CHAPTER 48

As soon as Naim stepped outside of the Daly Building, he stopped thinking about the attorney-client privilege that bound him to hold the secret of his client. That was a big problem. A tidal wave of reporters and cameramen rushing towards him was another one. They all shouted questions on top of each other.

"Mr. Butler, what's your client's name? The Judge Killer?"

"How can you represent a terrorist?"

"When are you going back to New York? No one wants you here."

"Who's paying for your services?"

"Has the killer killed anyone else?"

He was speechless for the second time in minutes. Naim squinted at the bright camera lights and ducked and weaved his way towards the curb. He was not one to shy away from the fireworks and flavor; but, David Thurman gave him a new bid to be more humble. An act that demanded delicious dedication. *Taking this case was a huge mistake,* he thought. An ample mistake quickly cascading into a tragedy.

Naim continued up the sidewalk trying to get to the Judiciary Square Red Line Metro train station. That was his smartest move from a menu of bad options. If there were seven minutes in heaven, he wanted a double.

CHAPTER 49

The sun was barely down, but Naim's day had already been darkened. Back at the hotel suite, he laid on the sofa with his head rested on Brandy's lap. Her delicate hands massaged his temples to counter a massive migraine. They awaited dinner from room service, but he had wanted to go out for supper. That morning, he had learned that his client was on the front page of a newspaper by way of room service. He no longer wanted their services. In fact, he wanted to be in New York consoling his son, and out of Washington coddling a bona fide murderer. A mass murderer. A lunatic.

On the television: "New York Senator Mac Donald, the Democratic presidential nominee had been recorded at a fundraising event calling the Republican nominee, Donna Lincoln unhinged and temperamentally unfit to be in command of the nuclear codes. This is undoubtedly unprecedented for a nominee to talk so recklessly about another candidate. The name calling is bizarre."

Brandy said, "Can you believe this? Your guy, Mac Donald, had better be careful. The more he bashes her, the more people may tune him out. He's attacking her mental health to be president. Bashing a woman will not work, even if a political foe."

"The last thing I want to hear about is mental health," Naim said, covering his face with two hands. "I'm disgusted. How'd I get myself into this?"

"Naim, he's crazy. Must be. A jury has to buy that. The people that he killed alone makes in clearly crazy. No sane person would do that no matter how angry they are with the politician."

"But I don't buy it."

"You don't have too. All you have to do is sell it."

"Easy for you to say. I'm the lawyer. You're the reporter."

"Hence, you don't have a conscious. You're blind like Lady Justice. She's blind as…Insert any cliche."

"You're kidding."

"I'm not. You're a very smart man. You fought hard to be a lawyer. Getting guilty people off is a line written on your doctorate diploma in imaginary ink. I read it myself."

"That is not true."

"Now it seems you're delusional. Or in the words of MacDonald: Unfit."

"The hell I am."

"Not literally, but, if not, what's the problem?"

"You're oversimplifying this, Brandy."

"I'm not. They have to prove his guilt. I was outside of that senator's home. They're not certain if the judge's and senator's home were hit by the same idiot. What if he didn't kill either?"

"He did it." Disbelief. He sat up and tossed his head back.

"And again, that's not your problem. They have to prove that."

"That's not fair justice."

"Now I'm scared. That doesn't exist. Nor does fairness. Perhaps, I've miss judge you."

"What's that supposed to mean?"

"Naim, black folks have been railroaded so frequently for so long its high time the country has a wake-up call. If I recall you were outraged weeks ago because a jury hung in a case where a white cop shot a black man running away from him six times in the back and ass. There was a video for Christ's sake. Consider Thurman as payback."

"News flash, he's white. The judge and senator were black."

"Skin color only matters to mask the retribution. Them two cock-suckers had bailed out of the black race forty years ago. You heard the room service woman this morning. Some people are celebrating the judge's death."

"I can't believe that I'm hearing this from you."

"You love me for being different. Tonight, you've learned how truly different I am," she said, listening to a knock at the door. "Dinner is here. Let's eat, rest up, and then hit a go-go club. It'll be fun."

"I'll get it," Naim chirped and jumped up from the sofa. Walking to the suite's door, he was shaking his head.

Naim opened the door and before him stood, Sinia Love.

Naim didn't flinch. True legal canons were so polite.

"Hi there," Sinia said, waltzing—uninvited—into the room gliding on water, flapping her lashes like feather dusters. Shifting her purse to her left shoulder, she held out her right hand in Brandy's face, and said, "So nice to meet you, Brandy."

Room service had struck again.

181

CHAPTER 50

In a room on the floor below, Malik el-Shabazz examined the listening device he'd planted to spy on the defense attorney and political newspaper editor. Perfectly hidden. Clandestinely installed. Perfunctorily recording. The Washington way.

To fully complete his mission he had to escape. El-Shabazz checked himself in the bathroom mirror and ran a brush through his ear-length brown hair, the tangled beard suggesting an Islamic bravo, a roisterer promoting a peck on the lips for a woman. It was his grand introduction, an act to make people aware that they were not all a batch of terrorists. He was a smidge under six-two, much of his face covered by the beard, and his eyes were dark, one may have considered them banishing and evil.

He was dressed in a pin-striped suit, white shirt, and blue tie: the basic D.C. raiment. Even his handkerchief was politically correct.

His cell phone, encrypted, beeped, Shai Brown said, "Come out, walk to the right, and I'm on Pennsylvania Avenue waiting. Gray Mercedes."

El-Shabazz didn't respond, simply switched off, went out, boarded an elevator to get out of there, a Panamanian woman smiled at the man who looked like somebody's favorite Bali-wood actor about him, expected he was an investigator for the sitting United States Attorney for the District of Columbia.

Exiting Trump International Hotel, el-Shabazz walked to the right and hopped into the waiting gray Mercedes.

Over the car's stereo system: "So nice to meet you, Brandy."

"You're just in time," said AUSA Brown. "Things are about to get a bit personal in the presidential suite. It seems," he said through chuckles, "that Mr. Butler has ran into his baby's mama."

CHAPTER 51

Brandy stood, firmly shook Sinia's hand, and smiled at Naim over the intruder's shoulder—that courtesy smile he recalled so vividly, the one that said everything was OK, even when she knew good and well that it wasn't.

"Goodness," Sinia said, her eyes darting, back and forth between the lovebirds. "You all look so confused."

Fact was, they were. A few months ago, Naim had promised Sinia to take good care of their son, Marco. She needn't worry, as he was in capable hands. Although he was eighteen, Naim had custody of the man-boy in New York, while Sinia lived in North Carolina. He also had a conditional agreement with Brandy to keep her away from Sinia. So far, he'd been good at doing that…Until tonight anyhow.

For peace sake, Naim smirked and furrowed his brows. To no one in particular, he said, "What a surprise."

"Sure it is," Sinia said, smiling now. "Hello, Brandy."

"Sinia," Brandy said. Her voice was sharp and clever. It could have been bubbling to a scorching boil. "Yes, what a surprise."

"Guilty as charged," she replied, smiling still. "Sorry to barge in."

"What brings you in town, how did you know where we were staying?" It was a tight and controlled compound question from Naim. He didn't want to sew divisions between the two women in any way.

"I will remind you, counselor, we share a son."

"Good, that's an easy one to correct. I can't have my son divulging my whereabouts to strangers."

"You've been in D.C. Three days too long. What are you going to sanction him like the president has done Russia?" She fiddled. "Isn't this a great election cycle?"

"Sinia, I'd love to talk politics with you. How 'bout we chat at the lobby bar?"

Brandy was looking at the exchange, her head whipping from left to right as if watching tennis match.

"Sure," she replied, walking towards the door.

He followed her, and said to Brandy, "I'll be back up in a sec. Before dinner arrives, in fact," before allowing the door to close behind him.

CHAPTER 52

"I'm the mother of your son, for God's sake! I can come where you are for anything. I'm not some media stalker or anyone like that."

Sinia was on defense the second that they sat at Benjamin Bar and Lounge. They had been having it out from the elevator to the bar.

"Sinia, there are rules and customs that we follow in this country. You don't pop up at my hotel and expect open—"

"I don't want to be in your arms. You must be mad," she snapped. "Brandy Scott teach you these customs. She parading around like step-mom and she's not even married."

"She's going to be and you need to get over that fact quick, hun."

"You're so full of it."

"Why're you here." He could tell that she was drowning, looking for an explanation for this surprise party.

"You left our child in New York. Shot."

He chortled to mask the disbelief. "Our child is in his first year of college. Second, our child has a nanny in the form of June. Third, my legal secretary and close confidante, Ginger, is also on duty. And Derrick's there in NY. He doesn't need me there. Where do you get this stuff? Acting like he's a toddler. If I need help with parenting I know where to find it."

"Apparently not. Your job seems more important than caring for him."

"I'm not going to do this with you. I talk to him three times per day. He has a security detail. I'm fundamentally opposed to you questioning my parental skills."

"You barely have them. You've been his dad for eight months."

"Your fault not mine. This is getting boring. I feel like you're trying to erode Brandy's trust in me."

"What happened to you contacting the feds to get my money back?"

He threw his eyes to the ceiling and tilted his hands back. "So that's why you're here?" He sat silent, before he said, "Using our son as a pawn. Ruining my credibility with Brandy and me."

"She doesn't even matter."

"Of all things I've said, all you decided to address is my reference to Brandy."

"Certainly she matters, I promise you that." He stood, pulled out his wallet, and tossed a twenty on the bar top for their cocktails. "I'm going to make a call to take care of that money issue tomorrow. In the meantime, I have dinner to get too. I have a huge case that I'm working on, I really can't deal with any drama."

CHAPTER 53

The next day was jam-packed for Naim as he choreographed his offensive actions. He honestly didn't give Brandy much thought working through the morning and, most of it slipped by the same way.

By noon he was sitting in a Baker and Keefe conference room, awaiting his team. He had the biography and resume of AUSA Shai Brown in front of him. The career prosecutor had grown into a sleek, tall gentleman with an Arab's bronzed allure, a man of high expectations and opportunity. Naim wanted to deny him any advancement, resulting from winning this case. Naim had an awareness of himself as being sharp-tongued, cynical, and keenly aware of the nature of prosecutors in general. He laughed because, Shai Brown, thought of him as an idiot. Strikingly sad and wickedly wrong.

When Margaret, Christina and Daniel filed into the room, they wore the same aloof mugs as the first day he'd met them. Naim e-mailed his team a memo of potential strategies that he wanted investigated, and he was certain that the efficient troika arrived to deliver.

"Did you all meet up before walking in here?" Naim asked, shaking their hands.

"No. Good time management. Noon means noon," replied Daniel Watts. He was in a brown suit with brown and mustard Cole Haan wingtips.

"OK," Naim said plainly. He didn't like the paralegal's tone. "Take seats and let's get started."

The secretary slid a folder across the table to Naim and both paralegals. "Just before I came up here, the indictment was filed on PACER. I've printed you all a copy of it, and it's in the folder. Included therein is the charged statues from Title 18, for quick reference."

"Thank you," Naim said, watching the paralegals at work on iPads.

"One more thing," Margaret said, her thick eyebrows rising to the sky. "Shai, presented the judge with an application for a search warrant pursuant to Rule 41 of the Federal Rules of Criminal Procedure and Title 18 Section 2703(a), (b) and (c) to compel Facebook, Inc. to disclose certain records and contents of electronic communications relating to the Facebook account identified by the username: David Goliath Thurman. I've printed the affidavit, and there's an emergency hearing set for two o'clock today, as they want the Facebook data to bolster the idea that Thurman should be detained without bail, so they need the info for a detention hearing,"

"Bullshit," Christina said. "This is a cheap ploy to get data for trial to establish premeditation for the murders."

"Couldn't we simply waive the detention hearing or stipulated to detention at arraignment, making the warrant moot?" Naim asked.

"You could try," Daniel said, "but that'll be Thurman's call. There may not be anything there, and he'd lose the opportunity for bail in the future if this case doesn't go to trial in say two years."

"Well, I will briefly chat with him before I lead to the hearing, so we need to speed this up," Naim said, flipping through the indictment. "You guys correctly surmised the charges. But, I see that the indictment lacks an overt acts section. As predicted we have six counts of murder of an officer and employee of the U.S. One count of first-degree murder. Two counts of attempted murder. Two counts of discharging of firearm during a crime of violence. Are the senator's and justice's security details covered by Section 1114?"

"Yes, they were not department store doormen. They were deputy U.S. marshals, according to the indictment." They're within the ambit of federal officers covered by 1111 and 1114, according to *Lucus v. United States,* a D.C. Circuit case, dating back to 1977," said Christina. "More recently, though, the Third Circuit Court of Appeals ruled in *U.S. v. Torres* in 1998 that when Congress enacted 1114, Congress intended to safeguard others performing federal functions as well as federal officers. Similarly in 2011, the First Circuit held that a detective with a municipal police department who had been deputized as a special federal officer was within the purview if 1111 and 1114 in *U.S. v. Luna.* In short, everyone is count one through six applies."

"OK," Naim said, "what about them proving premeditation? Why couldn't he have want to talk or demand, and that escalated to murder. Heat of passion? I'm asking?"

Daniel scoffed, and said, "Absurd. No jury in D.C. will buy that, first of all. Second, he killed the guards before he even got to the Justice and Senator."

"First of all," Naim replied, "you don't know what a jury will buy with this charming face calling it that," causing a chuckle to escape from everyone. "Second, we have no idea if they can prove the order that he killed these people. I hate to sound so calloused, but he could have crept into the homes, killed the targets and got the guards on the way out. Or someone else killed them all. Or the agents were killed outside before he got there and he stepped over them and killed the man and woman of the house. Limitless possibilities."

"Let's not speculate too much here. I'll prepare a Motion for Bill of Particulars. We will be better served with absolutes. I can absolutely tell you," Christina began confidently, "that in establishing premeditation, the government is not required to show that Thurman deliberated for any particular length of time before perpetrating the murders. Two seconds will suffice. We have a dead Supreme Court justice, here folks."

"Good points," Naim said, "I absolutely know that murder is a specific intent crime. Proof that the deed was done with premeditation is necessary. This is why they've submitted this foolish warrant to acquire all of his FB content. They need to find something to establish premeditation. I frankly don't believe that they have absolute proof of that or that he even killed anyone. The ATM video cannot possibly be their only piece to connect him to his crime. But what *if* that is it?"

Daniel said, "You're on the right path, but don't forget the mental health angle. Premeditation may be amply found to exist where on the day of the murders, Thurman entered the home, mounted a flight of stairs that led directly to the justice's bedroom. Literally stalked the victims in their home. Carried a murder weapon. And upon finding the victims, coolly took his knife and carved them up. The scene had handcuffs, will they be proven to be his. This case needs a savior, and a mental health defense is your Superman because only an insane person planned and did these acts."

Margaret added, "You have an appointment tomorrow in New York with Dr. Todd Rothman. He received his psychiatric training at St. Luke's Roosevelt Hospital Center in New York as a Fellow of the Columbia University College of Physicians Board of Psychiatry and Neurology. He's a long-standing member of The American Psychiatric Association. Since 1987 to be precise."

"I assure you," Daniel said, smiling, "In a prosecution under 1111, testimony of several psychiatrists that Thurman, at the time of commission of these murders, was schizophrenic and had no awareness of rightness or wrongness of his act, which evidence is substantial and reasonably impressive, will place a heavy burden on the government of proving that Thurman was sane beyond a reasonable doubt at the time the crimes were committed."

"But they'll say he was a smart, happy-go-lucky kinda guy," Naim said. "They've interacted with him at Capitol Hill and on the Supreme Court's steps."

"And not one iota of that will be sufficient to support a finding of sanity by a jury where there is a complete absence of evidence showing he was sane at the critical time when the killing occurred." Daniel removed his glasses, before moving on. "We're going to the emergency status hearing, and then, we're headed to visit the wife at jail. Visits are over at three, so Margaret while we're at court, we need you to contact the jail and inform them of our emergency visit."

"You all have this all figured out, I see," Naim said.

"We do," replied Christina.

"Behind every good lawyer is a great paralegal," said Daniel.

"And legal secretaries," Margaret said, forcing smiles to spread across everyone's face.

CHAPTER 54

Washington D.C.—National Mall

By one-thirty, Naim and Daniel walked down the National Mall under a bright sun. The sky was cloudless, the Washington Monument rising towards it like a missile being launched. Aside from the tourists and soccer players playing in the afternoon August air, they were just two men walking across the worn Mall grass.

"Daniel," Naim's voice was low serene. "Do you think I'm in over my head?" He hoped Daniel understood his question, because he'd hate to have to explain it at length. "I mean this is my first case and death is on the line."

"Shh," The fatherly old man clapped his hand on Naim's back. "You're a wise attorney. You're searching legal strategies, and that's what you have to begin with, before settling on one." They continued walking, and he said, "Pull yourself together. We're going to stroll into this courtroom, two strong and smart black men, who will sit in a federal court and defend a white man accused of murdering black politicians for their drug policies. Only in America, my friend."

Approaching the train station, there was an obese man in shorts and a tank top, reading a *Washington Post,* sitting on a lawn chair. He had a two-liter Pepsi by his side; an ode to the obvious coronary days from being unearthed.

Before Naim and Daniel passed him, fatty waved the newspaper and aggressively cleared his throat, grabbing their attention.

"Well, if it isn't the famous lawyer, Naim Butler," the man said, setting the newspaper on a patch of dirt. "Look at you on your sartorial best. What is the Armani?"

"Excused me," Naim said defensively, before Daniel put a hand up, preventing him from saying more.

"Here's a caveat," the man said, twisting the cap on his Pepsi. Huge hands titled the bottle to his lips, before taking several gulps.

"This ATM video the people claim to have used to target your client needs thorough scrutiny. You should get it. It may undermine their case."

"And you know this how?" Daniel asked, staring at the man. "This is Washington, sir. Call it a gift and keep it moving," the man replied, picking up the newspaper. "Ah, look, the DOW is up."

Daniel looked down at his watch, and said, "Come on, Mr. Butler, we have a hearing to get to." Before they entered the train station, he sent a text to Christina to begin drafting on a motion to have the government produce a copy of the ATM video.

CHAPTER 55

D.C. Superior Courthouse

"Thurman, you're the man," David Thurman said, referring to himself in the third person.

The murderer was being escorted from the attorney's interview room inside of the D.C. Superior Courthouse by Supervisory Detention Enforcement Officer Errol Clarkson. The top cop of the cell block was charged with moving Thurman back to a holding cell, before being transported to the D.C. Jail.

"Thurman mini-rant."

"Shut your fucking pie-hole," Officer Clarkson said, pulling Thurman forcefully by his arm restraints.

Thurman continued to shuffle along, slowly, because of the leg restraints. The Government had deemed him a threat to national security and instructed U.S. Marshals to guard him with force.

"I'm probably not going to be silenced," Thurman said, frowning and tilting his head to the side. "When I get out, and I am, what I am going to do, though, I'm going to put my dick in all three of your wife's pie holes."

Using a leg sweep action to demonstrate his disdain for the bloody killer, Officer Clarkson forced Thurman to fall face first and did not break his fall. Thurman let out a vicious howl, noticing blood on the concrete under his face.

"That's all you got," Thurman said, spitting out blood and a tooth, "you son-of-a-bitch. You're a dead man. I promise you that, Officer Clarkson."

Officer Dancy smelled the backlash, and radioed to control, "We need medical assistance in the cell clock, ASAP." He then turned to Officer Clarkson and said, "You need to get your story together immediately."

CHAPTER 56

E. Barrett Prettyman United States Courthouse

Naim Butler was a newcomer to the legal scene in Washington, though the firm of Baker & Keefe had an excellent name for itself. Naim and his paralegal assistant were at the E. Barrett Prettyman U.S Courthouse prepared to carve up the prosecution and officially make Naim's debut with his first court appearance as lead counsel. The change from his usual New York scenery wasn't apparent, thanks to the uniform decor of a federal district court in anywhere, U.S.A.

Naim was reminded of his first day at the University of Pennsylvania Law School, where he was determined to be himself. The same held true today. He had worn baggy jeans and T-shirts to class, bopped to rap music screaming through earphones while walking through campus. The first of his family to attend college, he was just an ordinary African-American from the ghetto, attending the nation's number one law school, and refused to lose his identity to fit in with some snobbish classmates.

Honorable Milton Hardiman was a beefy, broad rectangular man, built like a retired NFL offensive lineman beyond his prime. Quite a big man, a little fit for fifty-three, and he didn't look his age. He had hair growing on his knuckles and out of his ears. Balding, but he had a nice brown combover going, with kind deep brown eyes to match. His brows were thick and kept migrating to the bridge of his slim nose, as he studied the direction and nuance of the government's argument. He was greedily writing on yellow legal pad, as if the entire affair were an academic exercise of which he wanted an "A". The softest aspect of his face was his disarming smile, causing deep dimples. Naim knew that the smile was a lie.

AUSA Shai Brown, a career prosecutor, and no man's fool, was laying out the grounds for his need to have his warrant approved with surgical precision. He was careful not to drop bits and pieces about his actual case against David Thurman, and that was what Naim mentally prepared to capitalize on.

The prosecutor was up in the middle of the well at a lectern, in the closed courtroom, like a miser guarding information in the Information Age, but he had to light at minimum a small fire around the edges of their case to have the warrant approved. He spoke at a glacial pace and Naim presumed he was the kind of man that would pull a fast one if no one paid attention to what he said; a grave mistake that the rookie defense attorney wouldn't make.

Continuing his presentation, ASUA Brown said, "As part of our investigation into the mass murder of seven people and the brutal assault of two women, perpetrated by David Thurman, the Government learned that Thurman has a Facebook account where he posted long statements about his perspectives on life and would write about those things or people who bothered him. Most postings were depressing and negative in nature and could be described as mini-rants. The application for a search warrant was intended to operate in bifurcated manner. The Government outlined information that it wanted Facebook to disclose and specified the information that it would seize, both of which will be beneficial to the Government and the defense." And on that note he had a seat as if dropping the mic, because he offered the defense information on an olive branch.

Naim wasn't convinced and didn't need the prosecutors' help.

Judge Hardiman sat his pen down and looked at Naim. He said, "First of all, welcome to the D.C. District Court, Mr. Butler. Hopefully, you've been treated well, thus far, despite what you're here to do. And that is garner an acquittal for a man accused of murdering a U.S. Senator and a U.S. Supreme Court Justice."

Naim smiled, stood and replied, "Thank you." Whether the judge had shot at him or genuinely welcomed him, was a question he'd answer as the proceedings continued.

"I'm going to surmise that you disagree with the Government."

"I do, Your Honor," Naim said, proceeding to the lectern without notes.

"Proceed."

"Well, Your Honor, I prepared remarks, but they may not be relevant, considering the Governments request asks for material that do not support murder allegations. Here, today, Mr. Brown offered that my client, David Thurman, made so-called mini-rants on his Facebook page. However, the Government didn't outline any rant leading to the conclusion that Mr. Thurman desired to kill anyone named in the indictment, or otherwise. The prosecutor doesn't even indicate that any of the deceased names or their positions on government were ever mentioned in a Facebook post, for that matter. I'd be happy to take a look at any specific posts making this warrant necessary."

"He makes a good point, Mr. Brown. You say what?" The judge asked.

"Your Honor, while the defendant didn't mention anyone by name, he referenced senators and judges from all levels of our court system."

"None of them by name?"

"No, Judge Hardiman, but we can assume…"

"We can't," Naim blurted.

"Pardon, but I'm talking," AUSA Brown said, smirking.

"But we can assume that he meant the two deceased as one, the senator, championed the drug laws that led to Thurman's wife being sentenced to a mandatory sentence. The deceased justice wrote the opinion upholding the constitutionality of said mandatory sentence. No, he didn't day Judge Elberg, but it's clear who he ranted about."

The Judge nodded and looked back at defense counsel.

"It's *not* clear. Look…" Naim said, catching himself. *Calm down.* "Your honor, even if we accept the Government's alternative fact, as no one here knows who Thurman referenced. Their requested warrant is severely overboard, evades the fundamental requirement that a search warrant particularly describe what items are to be seized, and despite the Government's statement here, it fails the necessity of showing that the items seized are contraband, instruments of committing a crime, or evidence of a crime's commission. I mean, they're asked for things as mundane as pending friend requests, all posts that he used the 'Like" feature, and all privacy settings, to name some of the twenty. We're prepared to view all questionable posts and stipulate to the ones that aid the Government's case. That should be sufficient for the Government to make a bail argument, as their very general search warrant precipitated the enactment of the Fourth Amendment." Naim retreated to the defense table and sat.

"Way to point out your first point," Daniel whispered to Naim.

"Here's where we are," the judge said, flipping to a clean page on his legal pad. "The Government asks for the defendant's passwords, but if Facebook hands over the data, I can't see why that'll be necessary. They ask for security questions and answers, friend's list, future and past event posting, pokes, gifts, comments, and the list goes on for some two pages. So much so that I am inclined to reign it in some. I agree with the defense that the warrant is overboard and somethings simply do not get us to intelligence leading to a murder conviction. I'm duty bound to limit Facebook's disclosure to information about Thurman's account and the content of messages that he sent and all wall posts. I'll order Facebook to disclose records of communication, but not the content of communication, between third parties and Thurman's account. The Government is permitted to seize only the information directly related to its investigation. All records and content that the Government determines are not within the scope of the investigation, must either be returned to Facebook, Inc., or, if copies, physical or electronic, destroyed.

"A memorandum opinion will follow to explain the Court's reasoning for issuing the modified search and seizure warrant. At bottom, the Government's request is overbroad under the Fourth Amendment because of the unwarranted invasion into the privacy of third parties. If that is all, we're adjourned."

The judge skated from the bench as the attorneys stuffed their briefcases with their papers. Naim stood turned to leave the courtroom, and was accosted by the opposition.

"I gotta say good job."

Naim nodded. He didn't need a pat on his back.

"And your client is well trained. He hasn't said a word."

"And he won't."

"Wanna plead this?"

Naim chuckled.

"Remember you asked for this."

"No love, just sex."

CHAPTER 57

Trump International Hotel

To the Citizens of these United States of America:

Here's the bottom line, there are blood sucking vampires in Washington. They swing into town on the veins of their constituents, pilfer gallons of blood from the people's coffers, and die, leaving behind old money. I am here to get rid of them before they get to phase two of their wickedness. The Chief Justice and senator, the two dead ones, figuratively stabbed in the heart, the only way to kill vamps, were nothing more than warnings. More deaths to come, just so you know there are plenty of vampires in this town, a city which I've likened to a bat cave. Yes, D.C., the cave...LOL. No one, not one of them can complain of not being warned, although, they continue to enact laws that the people they're set to effect have no idea they exist or affect them. Well, I'm the new leader of the kill squad. To all of you blood-thirsty, worthless, SOB's, know that you're on notice. I'm coming. Either get a huge dose of holy water and change your ways, or die. I have to protect the American people.

Very yours,

A Killer Citizen

Brandy pressed her hand against the edge of the hotel bedroom desk, forcing herself away from her laptop. She stood as the chair she sat in flipped over. "Naim, come take a look at this. You think this is real?"

He was packing to head to the prison and back to New York. After reading the e-mail, he said, "Hmm, I can't be sure. You're a fine reporter that dropped photos of dead justice online," he replied and heard a ding from the computer. "Killers trust you."

"Shut up. I got another e-mail," she said, and pulled up a second e-mail. "And it's from the same account."

P.S. For the real press, know that this is not fake news. Believe me! The MPD will confirm that I carved up, stabbed in the heart, and handcuffed two vampires. Off to hell, they went. There's a new Secretary of Homeland Security, and all perpetrators of crime against humanity will continue to be blessed with Chanel bracelets and jailed in hell.

Brandy picked up the chair and sat at the desk. "Should I contact the FBI Cyber Unit or detective's pursuing the killers on this case?" The reporter asked the lawyer.

"No, I'll do it. Forward the e-mail to me to give me a leg to stand on while I put my other one up Shai Brown's ass."

"Whoa, be nice, my friend," she replied, laughing and forwarding the e-mail.

"Oh, this is me being very nice," he said, pulling his laptop from his briefcase. "But, you doll, have breaking news to report."

"You want me to publish this?"

"Of course. There's a jury pool out there, so get to verifying, or whatever, and break *your* story."

CHAPTER 58

As soon as Detective McGee got the word on the *New York Times* breaking story, regarding the threatening e-mails, she consulted with FBI Agent Morgan, who put her in contact with FBI Special Agent Linda Howe at the Bureau's Cyber Unit. SA Howe and Detectives Bald Eagle and McGee stormed into the Trump International Hotel. Within minutes of flashing badges, they showed up at the door of the presidential suite and were let in by Naim Butler.

"You look upset, but I had and still have a right to publish the article," Brandy said, as an introduction.

"It's called the First Amendment," Naim added.

"Can we take seats?" Detective Bald Eagle asked. "Where's the laptop you opened and first read the e-mail?" She asked sitting on the sofa with her colleagues.

"Why?" Brandy asked.

The detective waved a well-manicured hand at SA Howe. "Meet FBI Special Agent Howe from the Cyber Unit. She's going to work with you to determined where the e-mail originated."

"No, she's not," Naim said. "How'd you even know we were staying here? Our room isn't in either of our names."

"Mr. Butler, I'm with the FBI, one. Two you're in D.C. And, three, we have a dead SC Justice and Senator. Do you really believe that you've blown into town to defend their murderer and no one has your temporary address? You're missing a helluva game, if so."

After carefully digesting her words, he begrudgingly snatched up the laptop walked into the bathroom and tossed it into the sink. With shower water running, he walked back into the living room.

To the cops, he said "You can't look through her laptop as her sources, methods, and data are protected. You can chat with her and she can tell you what she wants too, but make it quick, I've still got a lot to do today."

"You know, you're an ass," Detective Bald Eagle said.

"Why thank you, ma'am," he replied, smiling.

"This is a murder investigation. If there is another killer out there we need to know. Perhaps this is a copycat. Or an accomplice."

"Or the actual perpetrator and my client is innocent."

"Look, you have your splashy headline, but we need some cooperation on this."

"No problem," Brandy said, as if she wanted to welcome their questions without feeling like they were injecting her with cancer. A lot of cops—and federal agents—tended to regard reporters as an obstacle than an ally searching for the truth. They wanted her intelligence and she would oblige to an extent. "Let me state the obvious. I got the emailers address dboxer@ussenate.com, which suggests Senator David Boxer sent it. That's doubtful. Maybe he was hacked by Russians and this is all a farce." She smirked, tucking hair behind her hair.

That caused a chuckle to come from Naim.

"This is not a game here. Sounds like you're a conservative, and if so, I hope you're not guiding the public to regard this killer as a hero, with your media megaphone."

Brandy smirked, "Pathetic," she said. "I've got a degree from U Conn, my integrity had never been questioned, and my articles have never been deemed biased. I don't have to make the killer a hero, because whoever he may be is. A direct correlation to the unpopular victims. The fame is undeniable, and anyone with balls will have the temerity to admit that."

SA Howe was taken aback. "Nine dead, and the killer is being admired. Our country is in bad shape."

"No, it's just tired of politically correct hogwash. It's why the unhinged and disrespectful, Donna Lincoln, is the Republican candidate for president. She disrupts the term *presidential* and people love that. Politicians have been putting on suits and lying to the American people with *presidential* customary behavior, like the deceased for decades. She's refreshing. The two dead men have been deemed oppressors of their own race. Many blacks wanted them to croak. So no one should be surprised that there are cheers in the street now that they're gone. Liberals in the Congressional Black Caucus scream about mass incarceration when they voted *yes* to enact the laws that created it. And now they pretend to be surprised by the murders. I report *facts* and unbiased news the people can use and, these e-mails suggest there's another killer out there hunting vampires. I put the blood-suckers on notice. You're welcome." She shrugged.

Brandy was on the defense, unleashing her fury. Being questioned by the police was not something she liked, and she wouldn't put up with it. No way she'd take their presence as anything but a fight. She was in her corner gloved and waiting for the bell to sound.

"We need to know where the e-mail was sent from. The computer. The location."

"I doubt the U.S. Attorney will agree that this is a protected source. Or a judge signing the warrant to go through your e-mails. We do that, we can and will learn far more about your sources than you desire. How do you want to do this?"

"Sounds like a good idea. And we'll ignore charging Naim with obstruction for trying to destroy the laptop. Water is no real match for our forensics team, by the way," Detective McGee said. "You give up the IP address and we're outta your hair. Didn't you say something about having to be somewhere?"

As they tried convincing Brandy to give up her source, Naim was in a heated text exchange with paralegal, Christina Gordon. Putting the phone into his pocket, he said, "Listen folks, we have the IP address. Get a warrant and well gladly turn it and anything else the judge directs us to turn over. The warrant is for the optics. I'm sure you understand that she can't give up to cops and not jeopardize her career. I'll see you out now."

The police stood in unison.

"We can see ourselves out," Detective McGee said, handing Brandy a business card. "If you leave town before we confiscate the laptop, please let us know."

Detective Bald Eagle said, "Yes please do go back to New York. We'd love to invade your comfy Eighth Avenue office. I'm sure there will lots of material there for us to confiscate."

When they left the room, Naim opened the door and stood in the doorway until the cops entered the elevator. He then retreated into the room, wearing a look of defeat.

"What's wrong?"

"There's a problem. As I told you earlier, I had my secretary contact the jail to request an emergency visit after visiting hours to meet with Jillian Thurman to get family and psychological background info on David. The warden OK'd that, but she just received a call from the warden's assistant that the approval was reversed. Because of a public safety exception, she's been placed in the hole and not allowed visits from anyone until further notice, per—"

"AUSA Shai Brown."

"Yes."

"How the hell did he even know you were going there?"

"Apparently, my dear, there's a leak in my faucet," he said, walking to the bathroom.

"Where are you going?"

"I need a drink, but first lemme get your laptop. I tossed it in the sink and turned on the shower water."

"You crafty son-of-bitch."

CHAPTER 59

Washington, D.C.—George University Hospital

MPD Detectives put in a bout of late-afternoon meetings and brainstorming sessions with their captain at the Daly Building. They planned how to bring David Thurman to justice.

Gas chamber.

Electric chair.

Firing squad.

They used the time to complete affidavits and warrant drafts for AUSA Shai Brown to obtain authorization for them to execute. They agreed to meet at the D.C. Jail later that night. What a Thursday.

Walking into the Georgetown University Hospital, the staff knew that something was up when badges were pressed into their faces. They requested and was directed to the Critical Care Unit, before they were asked to wait for department head, Dr. Jack Cardo.

"Thanks for meeting with us on such short notice," Detective McGee said, extending her hand to the doctor when he appeared before her and Detective Bald Eagle.

They shook hands. Dr. Cardo said, "So nice to finally meet you, Detective McGee. I was a fan of The Westwood Beat before they retired the show." He then turned to Detective Bald Eagle and shook her hand, "Thank you for your service." He began walking down the corridor and they followed.

Settling into his office, he said, "Let's get right to it because there's not much to cover."

"Right," Detective McGee said, "we need her official injuries to determine charges."

Detective Bald Eagle gladsomely added, "Like attempted murder or assault," with a grin.

"Both if you're asking me," the doctor said. "Definitely, the killer may not have intended to kill her. But surely, he knew, any sane person would know, the result of a stomping foot on the face could result in death. But I assume that's the kind of intent finding for a jury."

"You assume right. But you're saying this wasn't a punch?"

"Definitely not. We have a boot print on her face."

"Un-freakin'-believable," Bald Eagle said, shaking her head.

"Very," the doctor replied. "Let me walk you through what I can testify to in court."

"Please."

"My residents were consulted shortly after, Joanne Weston, perceived preliminary CT scans and I ordered additional scans, which showed multiple broken bones in her face. Joanne's top jaw was broken off of her skull, and her cheekbone was broken into her top jaw. Given the location of the fractures. The sensory nerve runs under the eye and gives sensation to the face, lip, nose, front teeth and gums."

"How's this all being treated?"

"Well, that's a work in progress. Having seen the CT scans, we first provided antibiotic coverage to prevent infection and then to take nasal precaution to keep Joanne from blowing her nose and causing bacteria from the nose to blown into the tissues. Thereafter, I surgically wired the jaws together, taking care to align them anatomically, and then installed plates and screws to stabilize the segments." Before continuing, he sipped from an *I ♥ New York* mug, and pulled a photo from a folder on his desk, showing his captive audience. "Joanne had one incision on her face," he pointed at it, "one large incision in her mouth, with a plate at the left orbital rim to secure the top jaw back to the sill. Her jaw will remain wired shut for a few weeks to prevent the bones from moving, allowing them to heal and preventing infection."

CHAPTER 60

D.C Jail Mental Health Unit

"If you want a Code Blue conflict in here or some fireworks and flavor, try sticking that needle in me. Violence, I don't shy away from it," David Thurman told the duty nurse.

During his intake health evaluation, clinicians informed Thurman that, according to test results, he was diabetic and that they would administer medication to treat the condition. Thurman had repeatedly denied having diabetes, refusing medication, and dared nursing staff to alert a squad of COs—known as a "code blue"—dedicated to restoring order about his defiance.

"Listen, just cooperate and avoid being physically restrained while we inject you," the nurse suggested. Her tone exuded bleak enthusiasm. Nurse Terrano was tall. thirty-six-year-old, practitioner, who wore reading glasses, thick blond hair hanging off her tanned face, flashing a movie-star smile.

"We've been over that. Bring it on, bitch."

"Remember that you asked for this," Nurse Terrano replied, picking up a phone.

"Wait." Urgent reconsideration.

"You're willing to comply." The only option.

"Maybe I need your help."

"With?"

"Getting out of here."

"As in helping you escape?"

"Don't get all indignant on me. As long as they build prisons someone will try to escape from them. But I don't want that. All I want is for you to call my lawyer and tell him to come here immediately. They're going to kill me. I don't have diabetes. I'm not crazy, either. Look at my face. They did this to me as an appetizer. Now they've locked me in a mental health unit to not be able to ask other inmates to help me. I'm not a killer. Please. Just call him, please." The entree.

And I'd hate to see desert.

"I can't do that."

"Can you for twenty thousand dollars?"

CHAPTER 61

Chevy Chase, Washington, D.C.—St. John's College High School

Football practice had ended some hours ago, but the Thursday night lights still shined over the field at St. John's. The lights stayed on until five a.m. as a deterrent for people searching for a place to make out late night behind the bleachers. What about clandestine meetings between a defense attorney and his private investigator? The Christian military high school was the perfect place for this sort of get together.

Naim Butler stood in the entryway, waiting for Jason Porter. He'd driven around the affluent Chevy Chase neighborhood of Washington, D.C. for a half-hour, assuring that no one-tailed them from the hotel, before Porter dropped Naim at the field's gates to find parking. It was eleven p.m. and they were trespassing, but as Porter's alma mater, where he was a star tight-end, he could explain the late-night visit.

Porter walked up to Naim, carrying a six-pack of beer.

"Sam Adams? You think we need cold-ones for this?" Naim asked, walking towards the bleachers. He couldn't help but laugh.

"Cover, my friend," he said, revealing a book in his other hand. "Also for our cover my yearbook. Class of 1992. This is Washington. You have to use CIA operative tactics to survive the city's treachery. This isn't New York. It's worse."

"Indeed," Naim said, copping a squat in the stands on the ten-yard line. He wanted to be close to the exit in the event he had to make a hasty exit. His mood was clearer after reaching out to his college pal. He hoped porter could he help him see the world in a different light.

Investigator Jason Porter was born into an Irish family in Boston, Massachusetts with spicy mustard color hair, green eyes, and a solid physique. A forty-two, he had sixteen years of helping lawyers solve crimes, starting with the Washington U.S. Attorney's office, later a CIA analyst, both after graduating from Tulane University a few years before Naim.

"I think there's a leak coming from my camp at the Baker and Keefe Washington Office."

"Could you run that by me again?" Porter asked, popping the top off of a beer bottle, taking a swig. "In English this time 'round, mate."

"I had been scheduled to meet with my client's wife at the women's prison in West Virginia. It was mysteriously canceled. And I was blocked from visiting her." Naim looked at Porter. "The only people with knowledge of my appearance were my D.C. B and K team. Two paralegals and secretary." Naim pulled a slip of paper from his pocket and passed it to Porter. "Their names."

"These sort of intelligence investigations have consequences," Porter said, remembering the years he's spent in the prosecutor's office. "You're looking to call someone out for being a traitor. And I am assuming you've asked no one about the leak idea. If you're wrong and it's not them, you lose your team. And respect. Such a Catch-22."

Naim rubbed his temples. The Samuel Adams suddenly looked appealing, though he hated the taste of beer.

Over the next fifteen-minutes, Naim filled him in on his mission and expressed how critical it was for it to succeed.

"I can see this being effective." Another swig. He stood.

"Sit. There's more."

"Ah, an encore."

"I was headed to New York tonight to meet with a psyche tomorrow, but I've secretly invited the doctor to D.C. without telling my team. Subterfuge feels horrible."

"It's not. But this ruins your shot to check up on Marco."

"Not quite. Him, his girlfriend, and my New York secretary are clandestinely headed here as we speak."

"Clever."

"I need you to investigate David Thurman, also. I want his military record, domestic and foreign travel, family, friends, favorite channel, favorite type of drawers. I want everything."

"I can do that."

"Can you get the owner of an IP address?"

"I can do that, too."

"What can't you do?"

"Golf."

Chuckling, Naim passed along another slip of paper. A check.

Porter looked at it. "You knew I'd say 'yes'?"

"Come on, mate. Do you think you'd be here if I thought otherwise."

CHAPTER 62

D.C. Jail

AUSA Shai Brown managed two lives: at the U.S. Attorney's office, he was a heavy-handed prosecutor as dedicated to his career and a NFL player—winning by any means, running right up to the out of bounds lines, conning the opposition with trick plays, mastering the art of creative aggressive prosecuting, and making a faithful husband to Natasha and a hero to Valentine, in whom he worked hard to instill in the teen the virtues of living a good and productive life. Natasha didn't want to know about his job, and she didn't like watching him on the news because Valentine didn't need to know the monsters that he prosecuted. He brought one thing home from work. Money.

It wasn't unusual for lawyers to mirror a Jekyll and Hyde lifestyle, effortlessly orchestrating a strong division between their double lives, outright lying to their spouses and children, and hiding their lawyer lives like a pastor in Los Angeles hiding illegal immigrants.

Shai always told people that he was simply a lawyer, not a prosecutor. Smartly, he left what he did at the office there. He walked into the office each morning and became a successful lawyer, he left each night and became a better man again. But with each night, the transformation back from Hyde to Jekyll became increasingly taxing. He fought it back because he couldn't allow his ruthless and spiteful ways to become known by his family. It was likely they'd leave him. Shai Brown had never brought his lawyer life home-never!—but he took it to the D.C. Jail with the masterful skill used for a NFL team to come back and win from a 28-3 halftime deficit.

D.C. Emergency Medical Service transported Thurman to George Washington Hospital, after his little accident. He received treatment for injuries—two broken teeth, a split lip, and two black eyes—sustained in the care of U.S. Marshals. During his time at the doctor's office, a clinician's assessment indicated that he had delusions of grandeur. Upon being discharged he was transferred to the Mental Health Unit of the District of Columbia Jail and dressed in an orange jumpsuit.

At 3:17 a.m. AUSA Shai Brown was behind a tinted glass watching detectives interrogate, David Thurman at the D.C. Jail. They'd been at it for six-hours, despite his injuries, with no intentions of stopping until they had a confession. There had been times when Shai hated his job, this morning wasn't one of them. He was enjoying the show. No popcorn needed. "You got your coffee. We've even accommodated you with a cigarette," Detective McGee said.

"Thank you, ladies."

"Now it's your turn."

"She's asking nicely. Screw that. We've kissed your ass. Now reciprocate," Detective Bald Eagle said.

"Bend over," Thurman said, flashing his new imperfect smile. Drawing her hand back, Detective Bald Eagle forced Thurman to slam his own forehead on the table, attempting to avoid her hit.

"Pussy," she said. "And sit up straight when women are taking to you."

Thurman wiggled his jaw, adjusting it. "That was strong enough to have broken my jaw. Luckily, I'm cuffed." He grinned wickedly, and then put the cigarette out on the table. "How's the jaw of Chief Justice Weston's wife?"

"What a sexist question. See, you can't even call her by name. She was nothing more than a judge's wife. Pathetic."

Thurman closed his eyes, using the three seconds to reboot from the interrogation. He refused to be—or even appear—broken by the worthless cops.

Detective Bald Eagle pulled her hair into a ponytail and rolled up her sleeves. "Joanne Weston fought you back. This I know. She sustained a large number of injuries to her hands and fingers—"

"Defensive wounds." Detective McGee threw in.

"Some that probably occurred while she was lying face-down on the floor with her hands covering her face. You can tell us what actually happened."

"We're going to be here a long time, if you want me to confess to these crimes. I did not stomp that woman in the face."

"Interesting, because we never said that you did stomp her in the face."

"What size shoe do you wear?"

"Fourteen," He grinned, winked and nodded towards his crotch.

"Good, the FBI Forensic Analysis team will compare all of the footwear found at your apartment to prints at the scene."

"So?"

"And we have your DNA," Detective Bald Eagle said, pulling the coffee cup and cigarette butt out of his reach, "which we will match to skin found under Joanne's fingers."

"Sounds like a frame-up job."

"Were you mad at the judge for anything?"

"Don't know the man. Never met him." He smiled.

"Your ASR website suggests otherwise."

"I'm not responsible for, nor privy, to all of the content found on the site. No proof that I've ever been on the site, by the way."

"There were weapons found at the apartment that you rented, too. Will one of the guns confess to the FBI Firearms-Toot marks unit that it fired the casing left at the scene?" Detective McGee asked.

Detective Bald Eagle followed up with, "You were military right? We believe a military-issued 9mm was used at least at Senator Elberg's. We're going to check to see if the serial numbers match any stolen military weapons. At minimum, yes, we will charge you with that."

"I was in the army, yes. Served this country honorably out of my ass. One honor that stands out is the Purple Heart. I have and will continue to protect the lives of all American citizens."

"And that's why you killed the justice and senator. Because of their laws and beliefs. You were protecting the American people. I get it."

"I didn't kill anyone."

"OK, put another way," Detective McGee Said, "you protected the people?

"Yes."

"And you did what you had to do to accomplish that. Confess and the people will understand. We live in a forgiven nation."

"No."

"You know that you're facing the death penalty?"

"It'll never happen."

"Because you're going to plead guilty in exchange for a life sentence?"

"No."

"You gunned down the security teams outside both homes?"

"No."

"Crept into both politician's homes?"

"No."

"Stalked the down the victims?"

"No."

"And stabbed them to death? You castrated the Justice?"

"He was caught banging a man in the ass with his wife in the garden, so, I hear." Thurman threw his handcuffed hand in the air. He said, "He deserved that, I'm sure. But I didn't do it."

"You saw him there, banging a man in the ass?" Detective Bald Eagle asked.

"Read it on a blog." *Nice try*, he thought.

"Which blog?"

"Can't recall. I subscribe to a lot of them."

"Can we get permission to check out your blog search history?"

"Don't think my lawyer will allow that."

"Actually, that's your call. You're a grown man and can negotiate for your own interests. Again, you're facing the death penalty, and I assure you that the Attorney General will sign off the authorize, Shai Brown, to peruse it. He needs a body for these murders."

"To hell with that crack-pot, Shai-fucking-Brown. He may be next on the killer's list." Defiant shrug.

CHAPTER 63

AUSA Shai Brown couldn't handle another ounce of bullshit being served by David Thurman. He walked into the interrogation room, quieting it. Sitting directly in front of Thurman, he raised an eyebrow, cocked his head to the side, and stared confidently at the defendant.

"You have something to say to God." His voice was hard, I-can-give-two-fucks kind of edge to it.

Thurman frowned and sat up straight.

"A minute ago you did, God particularly heard a threat," Shai said, looking at his watch. "At 4:28 a.m."

Thurman began to tremble.

"You see, I have my hands over your head with strings attached, controlling your life. Your every move. Everything about you. I, God, mutha fucking owns you," he said, asserting control.

Thurman coerced tears to fall from his eyes.

"A moment ago you were all locker-room-talk with the ladies. I'm only hearing sniffles."

Looking into Shai eyes, Thurman said, "I want to go home."

"Take responsibility for your crimes in exchange for life and you can go to USP Big Sandy and call that home."

"I want my dad. Why am I here in handcuffs? Are you a cop?"

"I'm in no mood for games. You're in boiling water and only I, God, can pull you out. Imagine yourself as the crab that you are, fighting for a way out of the pot."

Detective Bald Eagle added, "Listen. This thing wouldn't look any better with a telescope. It's a mess and it's your mess. Fix it with a confession."

"No more bodies," AUSA Brown said. "You've racked up enough, and someone—an accomplice, maybe—plans more, I guess. Tell us what you know, confess your wrong-doing and let me and my colleagues move on to the next case."

Thurman reached into the breast-pocket of his prison-issued orange jumpsuit, pulled out a card and sat it on the table. "My dad told me to call his friend if I was ever locked up. Please, can I call my dad's friend?"

AUSA Shai Brown picked up the business card of one, Naim Butler, Esq. "This is going to be a long night for you," the prosecutor said. "Give us a handwriting sample, lie-detector test, and let us test you for gun residue. And then, God will let you call your...um...dad's friend."

"OK," Thurman said childlike.

CHAPTER 64

The MPD and the federales didn't know shit. What they did know, though, was that Washington was becoming one vicious city and terrifying place to reside. This was not a typical Saturday morning.

Naim was pissed at the headline page A01 that morning screamed, **JUSTICE WESTON'S KILLER CONFESSES TO MURDER**, was proof that *Washington Post* didn't know shit either. Naim had forwarded to the prosecution an explicit directive not to interview or interrogate his client out of his presence. Ergo, the idea of there being a confession to anything, especially without his attorney in the room, was fake news.

The report had the same ol' story that media had been spinning all week: ATM video led to the suspect being featured on the news, identified by a D.C. citizen (unknown to the defense at the moment) tracked down, and arrested in a SUV at the MLK Monument. At a time when being a rat was at all time high, due impart to draconian sentences, Naim was not surprised that Thurman had been swiftly arrested.

Naim enjoyed the hoopla well enough, but he was sluggish with the constant media coverage and politicizing of his case. There was no question that his critical mission was to control the media slant as best he could so he sent out a press release. On the morning news, Thurman was a story and public enemy number one. Number two was a visit from the Russian government, and the fact that some diplomats were staying at the same hotel where Naim was taking up residence was just what he needed, *another story to get them capital L losers off my case.*

At eight-thirty there was a knock at the suite's door.

Brandy rolled over, her breast staring at him. "You expecting…Oh, never mind. Has to be Marco and company."

Walking to the suite door, Naim was impressed with his son's crafty exit for New York. Although, Naim had told him to take a late train to Washington, they had previously rehearsed that Marco was to fly if Naim told him to take the train and vice versa. After his call from Naim. Marco (with Amber and Ginger) walked into New York Penn Station at the Eighth Avenue entrance.

Exited on Seventh.

Checked into Hotel Pennsylvania using cash.

Checked out at five a.m.

Took a taxi to Laguardia International Airport.

And then, boarded a six-forty flight to Washington.

Now, in D.C. was the prince.

Naim checked the peephole, before opening the door.

Marco stood there, a smile on his face, with Amber and Ginger flanking him. All of them possessed overnight bags and dark sunglasses.

Ginger pressed her hand against Naim's shoulder, moving him to the side. "We're reporting for duty, sir," she said, stepping into the suite, followed by Marco and Amber. "But first, breakfast. No exceptions."

"None," Marco said, shaking his father's hand.

"Hello. Mr. Butler," Amber said, entering the room. "This is a lovely hotel. Good choice."

"That's to be expected at a Trump property," he replied, locking the door behind him.

Brandy walked out of the bedroom, fully dressed. Superwoman, no? "Hey, boys and girls," she said, grinning.

"Good morning, Brandy," Marco said and gave her a one-arm hug. His other arm remained in the sling.

"How's the arm?" Brandy asked him.

"Doc says its healing excellently. No broken bones," Marco replied. "But my stomach pangs from hunger is a whole different thing."

"Let me get myself together and we can go somewhere quickly," Naim said. "I have work to do sadly."

"Yup sadly, for you, dad, because us four have some fun and sightseeing to get too."

Naim wrapped his arm around Ginger, and said, "You three," pointing at Marco, Amber and Brady, "but Ginger will be with me conquering Washington, D. C."

CHAPTER 65

DuPont Circle, Washington D.C.—Busboys and Poets

This particular Friday after two of D.C.'s most influential political mavericks were killed was one of those rare gloom-ridden summer days —the kind where one could guess something was going to happen. In Washington something always happened. Hell, days earlier Senator Elberg was killed in his DuPont Circle home in Washington.

Naim Butler buttoned his blazer as he ambled—family in tow— from the security-driven armored SUV into the book cafe in the DuPont Circle neighborhood.

It was the kind of area to spend a lovely late morning with family, more mainstream on this side of the millennium—a trendy locale with coffee houses, restaurants, bars and upscale retail stores. The kind of area that kept the democratic liberal platform alive and kicking in America, just what conservatives needed to keep searching for their place in a country that legalized gay marriage, encouraged federally funded abortions and punished its citizens for not buying healthcare insurance.

Father and son, their girlfriends, and legal secretary were seated on the cafe's sidewalk patio. They ordered breakfast and drinks, before settling into small talk.

Although Naim and Marco father and son bond had only been brewing for eight months, their bromance was steaming. Naim reveled in the constant demonstration of Marco's reflection of him. Despite pushing through life just shy of eighteen-years not knowing the other existed, it was impossible to prove they hadn't been building together since Marco's birth. From their matching bushy eyebrows to their perfect SAT scores, to their musical talents, they were kin indeed.

Naim sipped his signature breakfast drink, a mimosa: his version 99% champagne and 1% orange juice. "How was the campus vigil?" he asked Marco and Amber.

She replied, "Sad. Very sad. I'm still lost for words that this man killed all of those students. And for no reason."

"And nearly me," Marco said, frowning. "But I am going to survive. Too bad the others didn't. Dad, you haven't missed anything being here in D.C. Not a dry eye on the campus all week."

"I can imagine and thankful that I'm not planning a funeral," Naim said, tossing a slice of bacon into his mouth. After swallowing and sipping his drink, he said, "I have a staff e-mail indicating classes will resume and/or begin Monday."

"As did I," Marco replied.

"Don't you have something else to tell your father?" Ginger asked, stuffing a slice of pineapple from her fruit salad into her mouth.

"I do," Marco said. "BMG called and informed me that they plan to have a certain artist record two of the sixteen songs from the compilation that I sold them."

"Who?" Brandy asked. "Should I be bragging about this to a lifestyle editor at the *Times*? Get you some coverage."

"You could," Marco replied nonchalantly. "I'm not ready for all this at but Winthrope personally called to tell me that Adele will do the songs."

"Wow," was all Naim could tell the music genius. "Congrats, son." Speechless.

"Thanks," he said, over the ringing of Naim's cell phone.

Naim said, "I have to take this," looking at the stern eye of Brandy. He was violating the No Cell Phones During Meals Act, but the unavailable caller could be his client calling from jail.

———————

The call wiped the smile off Naim's face. Everyone else's, too. The truth was hard to hide. His fingers trembled putting the phone back into his pocket. The phone dropped. It bounced off of the pavement and caromed between the curb and a car tire.

"Something terrible has happened at the jail. Thurman's been attacked by guards and shot up with something," Naim said, standing "I have to go." He picked up his phone, brushed it off, and waved at their driver. Pointing at his family, he demanded that he, "take them back to the hotel, and then meet me at the D.C. Jail."

Action and adventure spread across Ginger's face. "What do you want me to do, boss?"

"You my friend are coming with me. I can't trust anyone with a D.C. drivers license."

"Or Maryland, or Virginia," Brandy added.

"You three go back to the hotel, and stay there," Naim said. Raising an eyebrow, he looked sternly at Marco the one most likely to innocently defy him, "I mean it, Marco."

"OK, dad," Marco replied, "I got it."

Naim and Ginger jogged down the paved walkway, his long legs stretching like a greyhound. Vague sensations rushed through his body as if it didn't belong to him.

Hopping into a taxi on Connecticut Avenue, Naim gave instructions to the driver. He turned to Ginger, and said, "I'm not going to let these SOBs run me out of town."

"I didn't think so for a moment, sir," Ginger said, whipping around the DuPont Circle. "Glad to be here."

CHAPTER 66

D.C. Jail

Within twenty minutes they were beyond the earshot of guards, safely encased in a conference room the size of a cell, with the door closed.

"Who in the hell did this to you?" Naim asked, bearing down on his client, reddened tip of his nose, his voice leaking venom.

To Naim, a client may be a worthless piece of shit to everyone in the world, but he was Naim's piece of shit that was, and would remain the case.

"I don't know his name," Thurman said, looking at Ginger coyly, who was at the ready to pencil down his attacker's name. "I'm sorry."

"Why'd this happen?"

"He asked me to stop talking to another inmate," Thurman said, lying. "Apparently you're not allowed to talk during transport."

"Did you see a doctor?" Ginger asked.

"They sent me to the hospital. I could hear them crafting a story about me trying to escape." He shook his head, looking to the sky as if holding back tears. "They interrogated me over eight hours. Starting at ten at night. They shot me with truth serum. The nurse that called you, told me that. They told her to tell me that I have diabetes."

Naim was pacing the small room digesting every word from his client. He stopped, and said, "I sent an e-mail and letter via courier to Shai Brown demanding that they not interrogate you outside of my presence."

"He was there too. Bastard"

"Clearly out of line."

"He referred to himself as God."

Naim sighed. "I'm going to get you out of here."

"On bail, you mean?" Thurman asked child-like. "They promised me bail if I cooperated with them."

"They lied. A tactic they use all the time. They're going to contest bail. The judge will give them that wrapped in a bow. Especially if there's any incriminating speech on your Facebook page."

"It's not. Besides, they've drugged me."

"And at a hearing to suppress your so-called confession we will get that thrown out. In the meantime, though, I'm going to ask that you be housed in VA or Maryland."

"No, but, they have to be punished for tricking and drugging me."

"He does have a point," Ginger said. "I'm hearing all kinds of Amendment violations."

"Is that what you hear?" Naim asked, "we can't prove he wasn't given insulin."

"Yes the hell we can." In my presidential-slogan-voice. "The nurse would testify that she was also tricked into giving me a truth serum, forcing me to give a false confession. If I even did. I don't remember everything that I said, but I bet I said anything to get some sleep."

"Did you or did you not kill a judge and senator?" Ginger asked, scratching her head with the tip of a pencil as if she was trying to solve a college-level algebraic equation.

"That's irrelevant," Naim said quickly, his bushy eyebrows reaching for his hairline. "We don't ask clients that because the system requires prosecutors to prove that."

"On the stand they do," Thurman said.

"That's where the most lies are told in the courtroom," said Naim, smiling.

"And from the prosecutor's table," Ginger added. "Maybe not lies, but…"

"Alternative facts," Naim said. "And we don't call them lies. It's not polite."

"Spare me they politically correct, bullshit," Thurman said. "They're liars. What is our next move? Because look at my face,"—he tapped the newspaper that Naim had brought with him—"and the dumbass headlines on the cover of D.C.'s most read propaganda machine. The lying and manipulative prosecutor drugged me, coerced a confession out of me, and then artfully had the media run with his alternative renditions of the facts. That's the real fake news."

"They do have a media blower, but I came to D.C. with my very own media megaphone. I have to chat in-person with the nurse that called me. I wonder why she helped you?"

"I paid her twenty K."

"Wait. What?"

"This has bribery implications written all over it."

"But you should meet her. Nice piece of ass. You'd like her."

"Whoa. And the language," Naim said, rolling his eyes as if to say don't be a total ogre in front of the lady.

"Sorry," Thurman said, frowning. "It's true though." He smiled.

"One big bag of surprises is what this case is and I cannot take another," Naim said. "Are you sure you were injected with something other than medication?"

"It wasn't insulin, Naim why are you yelling at me?"

"I'm not," Naim replied cautiously. "I cannot walk into a courtroom and make bold statements that turn out to be wrong though."

"Nope, can't do that," Ginger said, "without Shai making him eat dog's ass. Fur and all."

The vivid image that Ginger had conjured up caused both men to smile.

"There's medical records to prove otherwise, Naim. Get them I'm ready to sign any authorization to get my medical records. I'm not a damn diabetic."

CHAPTER 67

Brandy was at the *New York Times'* Washington offices gathering intelligence so that she could write a column, of course, not to pump said information to defense counsel, Naim Butler.

At the hotel suite dining room table, over vodka and lemon cake, Naim and Ginger were discussing the Thurman case as it stood. He had filled her in about all that she's missed while in New York City, with Marco and Amber sitting on the living room sofa watching TV, listening to legal jargon-spewing from Naim's mouth.

"Very colorful week you've had I see," Ginger said when he took a breath and a much needed sip of coffee. "Far deeper than what's been in the news."

A BUTLER SUMMER

He nodded. "So what do you think of our celebrity? The notorious David Thurman."

"I'm convinced that had he not been stopped, he was on his way to becoming Charles Manson."

"No doubt. The fuckers been on the news every night. The lead story. His trusty press photo courtesy of the MPD photographers has gone viral. I'm baffled by the memes. Some people are glad that the universe has gotten rid of Elberg and Weston. And I have the sick pleasure of working to get the guy off." His manner of speech was didactic—practiced from lecturing and courtroom diatribe.

Finishing a bite of cake, she said "Lucky us," assuring her boss that she was on his team. She thought of a bible verse, St Luke Chapter 2 verse 23: *He that is not with me is against me.* She was undoubtedly with him.

He gave her a kind expression confirming his faith in her, despite his knowledge that they had a nutcase on their hands. "Still can't believe he convinced a prison nurse to call me. That or his injuries, I have to get him out of there."

"Well sir, he's a handsome man, that's a social media fact. So maybe she likes him. Have you read the comments on his mug shot posted on Facebook? You'd think he was Tom Cruise."

"Interesting.

"What do you think about our King David?"

"Just to keep the record straight, I think you're right that his phone is never on the hook, if you catch my drift. He's done how many Middle East tours?"

"He says 'two', but I have an investigator getting his whole record. He's going to check his US attorney office contacts to find out how Shai knew I was scheduled to visit Jillian Thurman. He's doing this off the grid, because I can't trust anyone in D.C. I know that they don't and they think they can control me with D.C. roadblocks. Ain't going to happen.

You're not the only one coming to D.C. from New York. I want my own team, not bought Washington insiders. This is frightening."

She chortled. "I'm not buying that it's frightening to you. You love this. Your tone, though, was straight-up. So much so, the jury might buy anything that you sell."

"I don't want to get that far. I need to put this puppy to bed before a trial."

"So, you have what in mind?"

"Interviews of David's father and wife. Prep for this arraignment and bail hearing are underway at the firm by aides. To my knowledge all the prosecution has is an ATM video allegedly showing David using the judges' debit card. David said he gave them a handwriting sample. I'm assuming that card may have had a credit card transactions requiring a signature to compare."

"That's OK, right, because you have his signature on the medical release form. And you can get an independent analysis, especially since you're going to introduce that he was drugged by the government's attorney and/or MPD detective's while giving the under duress sample."

"You have a point, A strong one."

"They've reported—the dishonest media—that he killed over laws that were designed to send his wife to jail for a mandatory term. I just can't believe he killed human beings over this matter."

"The simple truth, Gin, is people have been killed over much less." He shook his head. "If senators and judges are being slaughtered because people want stress free bills passed, there's going to be a lot of funerals in Washington. Every bill hurts someone. Period. There's a huge opioids epidemic right now."

"Yes, it's stunning."

"And I can tell you that if Donna Lincoln wins the election, penalties for the illegal sales of Xanax, Percocet and maybe even heroine will be hardened. People will praise her and Republican lawmakers for their effort to deter its use, which causes all of these media publicized overdoses. But as always the bulk of the new statutory punishments will disproportionately snag black people, and then comes the public outcry.

"Let's not forget that it wasn't a public health issue until it became a white issue. It was a lock they asses up issue when it was blacks and crack," Ginger said.

"So, again, every bill from criminal justice to medical care, someone will get hurt. There are three hundred twenty-five million people here. Imagine pleasing them all. Hence, David Thurman simply cannot kill politicians because he was one of the negatively affected. Can't please the world."

"Wait. Tax credits please," she said, smiling. "Everyone loves to get the healthy first-quarter government check. No disagreement there."

"Wrong you'll have people screaming that the wealthiest people got tax breaks, too."

"I'm not pleased right now," Marco said, laughing from across the suite. "All of this legal talk and political ideology and being confined to this suite makes me feel like I'm in prison."

"No doubt," Naim said, smiling. "Life sentence, with me as warden, 'cause you, my friend, won't be leaving my sight. Let's go downstairs for lunch, for now." He looked at Amber who was laughing, and to her, he said, "I don't know what's funny, hun. You have life, plus twenty years."